TOP-NOTCH DOCS

He's not just the boss, he's the best there is!

These heroes aren't just doctors,
they're life-savers.

These heroes aren't just surgeons,
they're skilled masters. Their talent and
reputation are admired by all.

These heroes are devoted to their patients.
They'll hold the littlest babies in their arms,
and melt the hearts of all who see.

These heroes aren't just medical professionals.
They're the men of your dreams.

He's not just the boss, he's the best there is!

Dear Reader

This is my second novel for Mills & Boon, and believe me it is just as exciting for me as getting my first one published.

It is such an honour to be part of a reading tradition that is a hundred years old. I can imagine our grandmothers and mothers reading the same romances through the years, and although times and settings have changed, the basics of a good romance are still the same—hunky men and gorgeous women that we know just have to be together.

I love writing romances because you can set them anywhere in the world. My husband, baby daughter and I spent fifteen months in Africa. While my husband—a doctor—looked after the patients, I looked after our daughter and taught part-time at a local school. Evening meals were taken communally, in 'staff house', and it was there I would listen to the doctors and aid workers discussing their days. I think back to the community often and wish we could have done even more. Things have improved a great deal since our time there, but there is still a lot that needs doing. So many children have lost their parents to HIV/AIDS. Therefore I plan to donate some of the earnings of this book to the children of Africa.

I hope you enjoy this story as much as I enjoyed writing it.

Best wishes

Anne Fraser

HER VERY SPECIAL BOSS

BY
ANNE FRASER

MILLS & BOON
Pure reading pleasure™

First published in Great Britain 2008
Large Print edition 2009
Harlequin Mills & Boon Limited,
Eton House, 18-24 Paradise Road,
Richmond, Surrey TW9 1SR

© Anne Fraser 2008

ISBN: 978 0 263 20493 3

Set in Times Roman 16½ on 20 pt.
17-0209-54299

Printed and bound in Great Britain
by CPI Antony Rowe, Chippenham, Wiltshire

Anne Fraser was born in Scotland, but brought up in South Africa. After she left school she returned to the birthplace of her parents, the remote Western Islands of Scotland. She left there to train as a nurse before going on to university to study English Literature. After the birth of her first child, she and her doctor husband travelled the world, working in rural Africa, Australia and Northern Canada. Anne still works in the health sector. To relax, she enjoys spending time with her family, reading, walking and travelling.

Recent titles by the same author:

DR CAMPBELL'S SECRET SON

To my husband Stewart
and all the doctors and nurses who work
in remote communities for no other reason
than the love of medicine.

CHAPTER ONE

KIRSTY kicked the tyre viciously and squealed in agony as a jolt of pain shot through her ankle. Damn, damn, damn, she cursed as she hopped around on one foot. Could this day—could her life—get any worse?

As if the twelve-hour journey in the cramped rear of the Jumbo hadn't been bad enough, the airline had lost her luggage. And then, instead of being collected, as she had anticipated, she had found that she had to make the five-hour journey to the hospital on her own in this heap of a car. Keys and directions had been left for her, along with a short note explaining that her driver had to be elsewhere and they would expect her before nightfall. It had taken her much longer than she'd anticipated to navigate herself onto the road heading north and she had found herself going in the wrong direction at least once. What sort of place was this she was going to that they couldn't be bothered to look after their new staff? What on earth had she let herself in for?

She was tired—no, scrap that, exhausted—and had planned to catch up on some sleep on the journey to the hospital. Instead, here she was in the middle of nowhere, under an endless African sky, with a flat tyre and no idea of how to go about changing it. Under these circumstances back home, she would have phoned road recovery to come to her aid or, failing that, some friend. But here she couldn't even call for help. She hadn't got around to converting her mobile phone so that it would work in this country.

Impatiently she swallowed the lump in her throat. *No use feeling sorry for yourself, girl,* she told herself. She gritted her teeth and studied the directions on the piece of paper in her hand. It looked as if the hospital was only three or four miles along the road—a walkable distance. The air was hot and turgid and Kirsty was aware that if she weren't careful her pale skin would burn. She should have worn jeans and walking boots, but she had wanted to make a good first impression, so had decided on a white linen blouse, skirt and heels instead. Her shoes with their delicate kitten heels might be the last thing in fashion, but they were no good for a long walk.

One last glance up and down the empty road confirmed what she suspected. She was going to have to complete the rest of the journey on foot. Kirsty had no idea when darkness would fall, but she guessed she'd better get going if she were to make the hospital in daylight.

Alternatively, she could stay in the car. Someone would come looking for her eventually, wouldn't they? But what if they didn't? Kirsty shivered at the thought of spending the night on her own. This country was too strange, too vast for her to feel safe, even within the locked doors of the car.

Grabbing her handbag and the tepid water bottle, she set off. The more time she wasted, the more likely it was that she would find herself walking in the dark.

The red dust beside the road coated her shoes as she walked and her ankle began to ache painfully. It was all Robbie's fault, she thought bitterly. If it weren't for him she'd never have made the journey to this godforsaken place.

An hour later and, although the sun was beginning to sink in the sky, it was still almost unbearably hot. Kirsty had finished the water and her tongue was beginning to stick to the roof of her mouth. Caked in sweat, she could taste the dust that seemed to cover her body from the tips of her toes to the top of her head. She had discarded her shoes and was walking gingerly on blistered feet. She felt her spirits lift for a moment as she saw the matchbox sized shapes of houses in the distance. Perhaps it was the village where the hospital was based? If not, at least there would be people whom she could ask for help.

Kirsty sat down on a rock and rubbed her feet. She would rest for a few moments, not much longer than five minutes, and then carry on. The chance of her reaching help before darkness fell was small but she also knew that once darkness came, her journey would be much more hazardous. Without streetlights, there would be nothing to guide her steps. An eerie cry in the distance brought her to her feet. Were there wild animals out here? Maybe she should have stayed with the car. Instead, she now risked getting mauled by a lion or some other wild animal.

After a short rest, Kirsty forced herself on. Despite walking for another age, the matchbox houses stayed matchbox size. Just when she thought she could walk no further, she saw the flash of sunlight on an approaching car in the distance. Please, let them stop, she prayed. At least if they wouldn't give her a lift they might have a phone she could use.

She almost cried with relief when the car slowed down before making a U-turn and coming to a stop beside her. The driver wound down the window and Kirsty found herself looking into a pair of glittering blue eyes.

'Dr Kirsty Boucher?' a deep voice said incredulously, adding before she could reply, 'Good grief, woman, what on earth are you up to?'

Relief that the occupant was someone who knew who she was gave way to annoyance. Did he, whoever he was, think she enjoyed walking in her bare feet in temperatures that surely must be close to 100 degrees? Did he think she was the archetypal mad Englishwoman? She opened her mouth to tell him as much when he turned his face and she noticed the scars that ran from his right ear to his jawbone. Years of medical training meant that she was able to disguise her shock, but perhaps not as well as she thought. Or maybe it was an instinctive response, but the man passed his hand over the scar before leaping out of the car and coming around to stand in front of her.

Kirsty felt dwarfed by his massive frame, despite being over five feet eight in her bare feet. She took an involuntary step backwards.

'I'm Greg. Greg du Toit,' he said, holding out his hand. 'We expected you hours ago. What happened?'

Kirsty's heart sank. This wasn't how she had imagined her first meeting with Dr du Toit, her new boss and the physician superintendent of the hospital. Somehow she had assumed he'd be much older. The man in front of her looked to be no more than thirty.

'Puncture, back a few miles,' was all Kirsty could manage through her dry mouth.

'And there wasn't a spare in the boot? Someone's head is going to roll. I tell them never to allow the cars to go out without checking. But come on, let's get you out of the heat.' For a moment he peered into Kirsty's face. 'And get you a drink of water. For God's sake, don't you know the first rule of Africa? Always carry plenty of water.'

Once again, Kirsty felt herself prickle with annoyance. He had no right to speak to her like she was some schoolgirl. OK, so she should have been able to change a tyre, but he *should* have ensured that the car she had been left was in better condition. Maybe for the time being she should let him believe that there hadn't been a spare tyre? No, she couldn't do that. If he found out, she would look an even greater idiot than she did already.

She sank gratefully into the cool seat of the four-by-four and she felt his eyes on her as she gulped greedily at the bottle of water he held out to her. When she had finally slaked her thirst she wiped the back of her hand across her mouth.

'There was a spare wheel. I, er...I couldn't remove the bolts,' she lied. Well, it wasn't exactly a lie. They were probably so rusted that she wouldn't have managed anyway. She glanced down at her perfectly manicured hands, which bore no evidence of having been anywhere near a toolbox, and quickly hid them under her thighs. It was only a white lie, she told herself. She just couldn't cope with this man's disdain. Not now. Not today. Her should-have-been wedding day. Swallowing hard, she pushed the thought away. She had promised herself she wouldn't think about it.

Greg glanced at his watch. 'How far back is the car? Are you up to going back for it? I don't want to leave it too long or we might find it stolen or dismantled by the time we get around to recovering it. We're pretty short of cars at the complex.' He smiled and all of a sudden the grim lines of his face relaxed. For the first time Kirsty looked at him properly. He really was quite attractive, if in a rugged sort of way, she admitted to herself. Not even the scar detracted from his looks. In an odd way, it even made him seem more vital somehow. Kirsty was already getting the distinct impression that this was a man who was used to people following his orders. Not that she would ever find another man attractive again—not after Robbie. Men were a thing of the past as far as she was concerned. She closed her eyes against the memories. She must stop thinking of the past and concentrate on the present. What was he suggesting? She stifled the protest that came to her lips. Go back? All she wanted was something to eat, a shower and a bed—and not necessarily in that order.

Still, Kirsty was painfully aware that the impression she had created so far was a million miles away from the one she had meant to make. Instead of the immaculately turned-out, efficient, career doctor she had hoped to present, here she was, bedraggled, dirt smeared and seemingly woefully unable to look after herself. Having to be rescued by her new boss had never been part of the plan.

'Of course we should go back. It shouldn't take long.' She straightened in her seat. 'I suppose they'll keep me some dinner?' She couldn't quite erase the plaintive note from her voice.

Once again she felt his appraisal. This time she was conscious of his gaze taking in her dishevelled appearance and her scratched and bleeding feet. He frowned as he started the car.

'Forgive me,' he said, steering the car back onto the road in the direction from which he'd come. 'You must be exhausted, as well as starving.' Again that brilliant flash of teeth. 'I'll take you to the hospital and come back with one of the others. We usually eat around seven. If we hurry, you'll just have enough time to freshen up before dinner. It'll mean waiting for your luggage, I'm afraid, but I'll bring it over as soon as I can.'

'There's no luggage,' Kirsty told him. 'It's been delayed. Lost somewhere between here and Timbuktu, I imagine. I'll have to find a way of collecting it from the airport tomorrow. Supposing they manage to find it.' She couldn't help sighing at the thought of a repeat journey the next day. But at least she'd have slept by then.

Greg muttered something under his breath that Kirsty suspected she wasn't supposed to hear. 'Bloody airlines. Still, it can't be helped. The driver who was supposed to pick you up, but decided not to come at the last minute, can collect it on his way tomorrow. I did try to contact you to tell you to find yourself a hotel for the night, but I couldn't get through on your mobile. I phoned the airport and they told me you had collected the car and were on your way. These roads aren't safe for a single woman, especially at night. When you didn't arrive by the time we expected you, I thought I'd better come looking. Just as well I did. You don't look as if you were in any shape to finish the journey on foot.'

Once again Kirsty felt chastised, although it was hardly her fault. Instead of apologising— after all, the car was the hospital's respon- sibility—the man was making it clear she was causing a lot of extra work.

'I'm sorry,' she said again, willing her voice to remain steady. 'I really didn't plan to cause all this bother.'

'No problem,' he said brusquely, but somehow Kirsty didn't believe him. She was beginning to think she had made a dreadful mistake in coming here. She wondered bleakly if she would be able to work with this man. He was far too autocratic for her liking and already seemed to have taken against her. But there was nothing she could do about it right now. She was far too tired to think logically so she closed her eyes and within minutes was fast asleep.

She was jolted from her dreams by the sound of an explosion. She opened her eyes to see a minibus swerve erratically across the road in front of them, bits of rubber flying from a rear tyre. Disorientated, Kirsty sat bolt upright in her seat and, as Greg veered to avoid the out-of-control vehicle in front of them, she spread her hands to brace herself for impact. For several breath-taking moments the minibus continued to career from one side of the road to the other, churning up clouds of dust in its wake before finally spinning off the road. Its front wheels hit a shallow ditch and Kirsty held her breath as, with the sound of crunching metal, the vehicle slowly tipped over on its side.

As Greg carefully brought his vehicle to a halt at the side of the road, Kirsty was immobilised with horror. She was barely conscious of him leaning across her to open the cubbyhole and scrabble for something inside, except, incongruously, the clean lemony smell of his skin.

'Double-glove before you do anything,' he said tossing an unopened pack of latex gloves onto her lap before reaching into the back for his medical bag. 'Let's go,' he ordered, and, without waiting for a response, was out of the car. Hastily, Kirsty pulled on the gloves and followed.

It all felt surreal to her. The music emanating from the vehicle's unbroken stereo system was a blast of happy sounds, a sharp, eerie contrast to the moaning and crying voices and the still-spinning wheels of the tilted minibus. Bodies spilled out and lay around, arms and legs twisted at unnatural angles. Still others were slowly extracting themselves from their seats and stumbling, zombie-like, away from the disaster.

Despite the warmth of the African sun on her bare arms, she shivered. *For God's sake,* she thought, *I've been in the country less than four hours and a doctor for not much longer. This can't possibly be happening.*

'Dr Boucher—Kirsty.' She became aware of a

hand on her arm and looked up into calm blue eyes. 'I have to phone for help. In the meantime you have to start triaging the casualties.' He turned from her and opened the boot of his car. He shoved a pile of lines and bags into her unwilling arms. 'Take this. Once you've finished triaging, put in lines where you need to.' She looked at him, still in shock. He shook her arm impatiently. 'Look, you can do this. I need you to help me.' He held her eyes for a few moments, and then with a final shake of her arm he was gone.

Out of the corner of her eye, Kirsty became aware of a small figure stumbling away from the wreck. A child, no older than two, toddled purposefully up the side of the ditch towards the road. It was the impetus she needed to shake her loose from the paralysis that had gripped her in the first dreadful minutes since the crash. 'Stop! Come back!' she called out. Tossing the equipment Greg had given her onto the passenger seat, she lunged for the child, grabbing the small bundle seconds before he reached the road. The frightened and bewildered child squirmed in her arms. She looked around at the passengers and, finding a woman who seemed uninjured, thrust her small charge into the woman's arms.

'Hold onto him. Don't let him go. Not even for a second.' She wasn't sure if the woman understood her words, but she must have understood her meaning as she engulfed the child in her embrace.

'Move away from the bus,' Kirsty instructed her. Still unclear whether the woman understood, she indicated a stretch of ground away from the bus and the road. 'Bus could explode,' she added miming an explosion with her arms. Thankfully the woman seemed to grasp enough of the exchange and moved away with her charge.

Kirsty retrieved the equipment Greg had given her and scrambled down the slope to the bus, oblivious to the small stones that scraped her bare legs and feet. The vehicle had come to rest at the bottom of the ditch, its front badly crumpled. The wheels on the driver's side had mounted a small hillock and the bus tilted precariously over to the left. The driver had been thrown through the windscreen and hung there like a casually tossed rag doll. Kirsty reached up and felt for a carotid pulse. As she suspected, the driver was dead.

Moving around the front of the bus, she attempted to open the passenger door. Unfortunately the angle of the bus prevented her from opening it more than a few inches. Through the narrow gap, she could see that there were two more people in the front seat—an elderly man, who was conscious and moaning with pain, and a young woman, who was crying but seemed uninjured. She recalled her training. *It's the quiet ones you have to worry about.* With these words ringing in her head, she decided that both casualties could wait until she had assessed the rest. 'You are going to be fine,' she said softly. 'I'll be back as soon as I can. In the meantime, try not to move.' With a final reassuring smile she left them and went to check up on the remainder of the passengers. Despite her initial impression, most of them seemed relatively unhurt, apart from possible fractures, lacerations and shock. They too could wait. 'I'll be back in a minute,' she promised the frightened and shocked figures. 'Those that can, move away from the bus. The rest of you, keep as still as you can.'

Leaving them she found Greg bent over a

young man in his early twenties, doing chest compressions. He had been joined by a middle-aged woman who, apart from a few cuts and bruises, seemed to have escaped from the minibus unscathed.

'This is Sister Matabele,' Dr du Toit said tersely, barely glancing at Kirsty 'She was on her way to work in a taxi when the accident happened. She'll help me here. You carry on treating the rest of the casualties. The paramedics should be here shortly.'

Before Kirsty had a chance to move, a voice called urgently. 'Help! Over here!'

She hurried over to where a man was cradling a woman on the ground a short distance from the wreckage. She bent over the woman who was lying pale and unconscious. 'My wife—she needs help. She was awake until just now. Now she is asleep. She is bleeding very badly from her leg, I think.'

Kirsty checked that the woman's breathing was unrestricted before examining her. Her pulse was rapid and weak. The heart was still beating, but only just. Swallowing her fear, she removed the

T-shirt the woman's husband had laid over the wound. Gently lifting the fabric, she revealed a hole the side of a child's fist at the top of her leg. Bright red femoral blood pulsed onto the ground.

Once again Kirsty felt the rising paralysis of her fear. *Keep calm,* she told herself. *You've dealt with worse than this before.* But that had been in the controlled environment of a large inner-city A and E department with the latest equipment and a team of experienced doctors and nurses. Nothing could have prepared her for this. She looked over for Dr du Toit, but he was still bent over his patient. For the time being she was on her own. These two people were depending on her. She needed to stop the bleeding, and soon. She placed her hand over the wound and pressed down hard. Her hand wasn't enough to stem the gushing flow of blood. She needed something bigger. A quick glance around told her there was only one option. Taking a deep breath to calm her shaking hands and to steady her voice, she slipped off her linen blouse, placing it onto the hole in the woman's leg. 'Hold this. Press down hard,' she instructed the

frightened man, taking his hand in hers to dem-
onstrate exactly what she wanted him to do.
Kirsty knew if the woman were to stand a
chance, she would have to replace the blood she
had lost with fluid as quickly as possible. Kirsty
used one of the lines she had been given and,
ripping off the protective cover from the needle
with her teeth, slipped the needle into a vein in
the arm. *Bingo!* she thought with some satisfaction as she hit the vein first time. 'What's your
wife's name?' she asked the distraught man.

'Maria. Is she going to be all right?' Kirsty
heard the fear in his voice. She smiled and kept
her voice low and calm. 'I'm sure she will be,' she
said, although she wasn't sure at all. 'Talk to her.
Let you know that you're here. Reassure her.'

As she worked on her patient, she felt a shadow
fall on her shoulders. She glanced up to find Greg
looking down at her. 'Are you OK?' he asked
from what seemed to be a great distance. 'Do you
need any help? My patient is breathing by
himself now. Thank God Sister Matabele was
here to help. She'll stay with him until the ambulances arrive.'

'This is Maria. She has a ruptured femoral artery. I've applied pressure and got a drip going. Her pulse and blood pressure are up, but we need to get her to hospital stat.'

Greg examined the woman briefly but expertly. 'She's doing fine for the time being. Good work,' he said warmly. 'I'll carry on assessing the rest. I'll let you know if I need you. But first…'

Kirsty felt him wrap something around her shoulders. 'Apart from the obvious distractions of a half-naked woman, you'll get sunburnt unless you cover up.' He smiled down at her and despite the situation, Kirsty could have sworn she saw a wicked twinkle in his eyes. Suddenly very aware that she was dressed only in her bra and skirt, the colour rose in her cheeks. Quickly she slipped her arms into the shirt. She needed to roll up the sleeves several times and it came well below the hem of her skirt. Her day was going from bad to worse. Now she was dressed like some kind of hobo. Never, in a month of Sundays, would she normally be found less than perfectly groomed. She shook her head impatiently. What was wrong with her? Thinking about clothes at a time like this!

'Someone! Please. Over here!' Another cry for help, but before Kirsty could react, Greg was already moving. Within seconds he was crouched beside the bus. A moment later he called out, 'I need assistance over here.'

There was little more Kirsty could do for Maria for the time being. In calm, measured tones she instructed her helper to keep pressure on the wound and, grabbing one of the uninjured passengers, told him to keep the bag of fluid raised. Once she was satisfied that her patient was in capable hands, she hurried over to Greg.

He was kneeling by the side of the bus, his mouth set in a grim line. The upper body of a young woman in her late teens or early twenties was visible from under the bus.

'This is Lydia,' Greg told Kirsty tersely. 'Her right leg is pinned underneath the bus.'

'I don't know how I missed her,' Kirsty said, upset.

'Hey, it's not your fault. You couldn't have known she was here. We need to give her some morphine and get some fluids into her while we work out how we can get her out.

'We're going to give you something for the pain,' Greg told the frightened young woman, taking a syringe of morphine from Kirsty. 'We'll have you out just as soon as we can.' While Greg administered the pain relief Kirsty set up a drip.

Large brown eyes darted from Greg to Kirsty. 'My son. I need to find my son. Please.' Lydia squirmed, trying to pull her leg from under the broken fender.

'Is your son a toddler of about two? Wearing a blue jumper?' Kirsty asked.

'Yes, yes. Did you see him? Is he all right?'

'He's perfectly fine. Someone's looking after him. We'll bring him over to you once we've got you sorted.'

Lydia's head sank back on the ground. 'Thank you,' she whispered gratefully, before closing her eyes.

Kirsty looked at Greg. 'How are we going to remove her safely?'

'The pressure from the bus on her leg is probably helping to stem the bleeding.' Greg said softly, his voice thoughtful. 'We'll wait until the ambulance gets here, then we'll have help to lift the bus. We'll need to be ready to control the bleeding.'

To Kirsty's relief, the wailing of sirens signalled the arrival of the ambulances. There were two, each with a paramedic. 'Tell the paramedics to deal with the injured, but get the drivers over here,' Greg told Kirsty.

As the paramedics set about seeing to the other patients, the two burly ambulance drivers came over to the wrecked minibus.

'OK, guys. Once I'm finished here, I need you to lift the bus. Kirsty, you keep the leg stabilised while I pull her out. Watch out for any sudden haemorrhage. It's quite possible the weight of the bus is preventing us from seeing any big bleeders, but once we lift it, that's when we'll know the true extent of her injuries. Get ready to apply pressure.'

Greg knelt and said something to the woman in a language Kirsty didn't understand. But whatever it was, it seemed to reassure her because she nodded and even managed a small smile.

At Greg's count of three the two ambulance drivers lifted the minibus, their muscles bunching with the effort. The vehicle was lifted a couple of inches, but it was just enough for Greg to gently pull Lydia out. Once she was clear, the men let the bus drop with gusty sighs of relief.

Although Lydia's leg was a mess, clearly broken several times with her tibia showing white through her ebony skin, the anticipated spurting that would indicate a torn artery failed to materialise. Kirsty breathed a sigh of relief and bent to cover the wounded leg with padding before stabilising it with one of the inflatable splints the ambulancemen had brought over.

'The rest of the patients are loaded and ready to go, apart from this one,' one ambulanceman informed the two doctors. 'The rest are walking wounded and one of the passers-by will bring them in by car.'

Greg looked at Kirsty and grinned, dimples appearing at either side of his mouth. His smile sent a shiver down her spine 'Good work. Not bad at all for a city girl.'

Kirsty felt inordinately pleased at his praise but before she could think of a reply he went on, 'I'll need to go in the ambulance with the two critical patients. Would you mind driving my car?'

'Wouldn't you prefer me to go in the ambulance?' Kirsty asked.

'I think you've had enough of a baptism by fire for the time being, don't you? The keys are in my car. Just follow the ambulance,' he said, continuing to supervise the loading of his patients. 'The hospital is only a few miles up the road. I'll see you there.'

Kirsty decided the easiest thing to do was to do as she was told. She hurried over to his Jeep and leapt in. She spent a couple of minutes familiarising herself with the vehicle. She had to move the seat at least a foot forward before she could reach the pedals.

Driving in convoy, they arrived at the hospital as evening descended. Kirsty was oblivious to the setting sun casting its halo of orange rays behind low, distant mountains. Instead, her only thoughts were for the accident victims and the doctor who'd worked so unstintingly to help them. What had caused the scarring on his face? It looked like burns. She had noticed that his right hand was also scarred, although the movement didn't seem impaired. Despite his rather cool manner, there was something about him that inspired confidence. Kirsty was sure he'd be a patient, if demanding teacher. She knew that if the rest of her new colleagues were half as skilled and dedicated as he was, she was going to find being part of the team an experience she wouldn't want to miss. For the first time she was really able to believe that coming to Africa might be so much more than simply running away from her past.

When the ambulance doors opened, a squad of staff surged around the injured. There wasn't time for introductions as Greg barked orders to them, instructing which patients needed to go immediately to Theatre and which required X-rays and tests before a proper diagnosis of the extent of their injuries could be determined.

'Jamie, take this one will you? Kirsty, give the boy to Sister Shange here. Elspeth, what's the status of the other casualties?'

'Would you like me to assist in Theatre?' Kirsty asked.

Greg stared at her, as if for a moment he couldn't remember who she was.

'I think you've done enough for the time being. We'll cope from here on. If you give me a minute, I'll find someone who can show you to your quarters.'

'But…' Kirsty started to protest.

Greg lifted a hand to stem the flow of words. 'I don't have time to argue. You don't know the layout of the department. Right now, we've enough staff to help. You'll only get in the way. Please,' he added firmly, 'leave it to us.' Then he smiled as if to soften his words.

Kirsty glared at him, her eyes flashing. He was treating her like some incompetent medical student.

Greg must have sensed her frustration. He raised an eyebrow at her. 'You did very well back there. Now go get some rest. You'll be in a better position to help tomorrow.' He turned his back to her, but not before something in those cool blue eyes told Kirsty it'd be useless to argue further. Reluctantly she looked at his retreating back.

Later that night as Greg wrote up his notes, he thought about Kirsty. The image of her standing before him in his bloodstained shirt and the short skirt which did nothing to hide her long slim legs kept intruding on his thoughts. She was undeniably attractive with her thick auburn hair escaping from her ponytail and her elfin face with those flashing green eyes. Although on the surface she appeared sophisticated, there was something vulnerable about her—and it wasn't just her age. He cursed under his breath. She had only been qualified for a couple of years. Despite the way she had performed at the accident scene, she was still far too inexperienced to work in such a remote and challenging setting. He had tried to refuse to accept her as a member of his new team, but had been overruled by the hospital manager. 'You can't keep working night and day, Greg,' he had said. 'This hospital should have twelve doctors, not the four we have. We need help, at least your colleagues do, and it's not as if we're overrun with applications to come and work here. You might be able to work all the hours God sends, but your colleagues need a break. If they don't get some time off, we could lose them.'

There was no denying his argument, but Greg knew to his cost that an inexperienced doctor could be worse than no doctor at all. With her delicate features and slim build, Kirsty looked as if she had just come out of medical school, although he knew that she was twenty-five. The last thing he needed was to babysit some inexperienced doctor who thought spending a few months in a rural hospital in Africa would be fun or, worse, a good way of practising newly acquired medical skills. He'd had enough of those types in the past and they had proved more of a hindrance than a help. Most of them had only stayed a short while. Long enough to realise that the incredibly long hours and hard work was too much.

He shook his head in frustration. He had been tempted to take Kirsty up on her offer of help earlier. Perhaps working through the night in the primitive and gruelling conditions would have been enough to see her immediate return to the UK. But the temptation had been fleeting. It wouldn't be in the best interests of the patients to have an exhausted and inexperienced doctor working on them. Still, he had to admit she had done well at the crash scene. Apart from that initial hesitation she had worked calmly and efficiently. He knew that more than one patient had reason to be glad she had been there. It didn't help that something in those luminescent green eyes had sparked feelings that he thought had gone for ever. No, it was best all round if she could be made to see that Africa wasn't for her.

CHAPTER TWO

THE sun streaming into her room woke Kirsty. Anxious that she'd overslept, she glanced at her watch and couldn't believe it wasn't quite six yet. She stretched, breathing in the unfamiliar but heady scents that drifted in from her open window. Last night, one of the kitchen staff had escorted her to her accommodation after serving her some mashed pumpkin and roast beef. The rest of the staff had all been busy with the aftermath of the accident, so it had been a solitary supper for Kirsty.

Although she had been a little disappointed not to meet and work alongside her new colleagues, part of her had been relieved to get the opportunity of a much-needed early night. She had barely managed to stay awake long enough to shower the blood, sweat and dust away, before collapsing into bed. She had expected to fall asleep the moment her head had hit the pillow, but instead had found herself replaying the events of the day and her introduction to the strangeness of this wild, untamed patch of Africa and its people, including the enigmatic Dr Greg du Toit. Although she couldn't say her new boss had been unwelcoming, she'd sensed he wasn't altogether happy to have her there. She had tossed and turned, wondering if she had made the right decision to come to work in this hospital deep in rural Africa. Would she cope? Everything seemed much more basic than she had imagined. But she'd had to get away. Put as much distance between herself and her memories as possible. She wanted—needed—to start afresh make a new life for herself. When at last she had fallen asleep, it had been to dream of Robbie. She had woken up to find tears drying on her cheeks.

But Kirsty was determined that today would be the beginning of her new life. Curious about her new home, she jumped out of bed. There was a set of scrubs on the rickety chair in the corner of the room. They hadn't been there the night before. Greg must have asked someone to bring them over. She was surprised that he had remembered, with so much going on.

The accommodation certainly wasn't lavish but, then, Kirsty hadn't expected it to be. Nevertheless she appreciated the gleaming polished earthen floors smelling faintly of lavender, cool and smooth under her bare feet. And although the furniture was sparse, she knew that with a few touches she could make her new home more appealing.

The house was at least half a century old, with a hodgepodge of additions over time to what must have been the original structure—a circular room from which a tiny scullery, her bedroom and a spartan bathroom led off at various angles, each serving to create interesting nooks and crannies.

The circular room—or rondavel as it was traditionally known—was divided down the middle by a freestanding granite unit that separated the living-room area from the kitchen. On closer inspection Kirsty realised it must have been an autopsy slab from bygone times. However, its antiquated, well-scrubbed appearance amused rather than repulsed her.

While the kettle boiled, she searched fruitlessly for something to eat. In hindsight, she remembered being told that staff meals were served daily in the dining room. If she preferred to prepare meals for herself, she'd have to do her own grocery shopping. Hell, there wasn't even tea or milk! Dispirited, she flicked the kettle off. Breakfast in the staff dining room it had to be!

She took a quick shower, pleased to find that while the furniture and fittings might be sparse, there was a plentiful supply of steaming hot water. However, she remembered that Africa often suffered severe water shortages and limited her shower to the minimum amount of time needed to soap her body and rinse the last of the dust from her long auburn hair.

She wasn't expected on duty until the following day but she was eager to see how the victims of yesterday's accident were faring so she dressed quickly in the scrubs, which were a surprisingly good fit. She wondered if Greg had selected them himself—if he had, he had an accurate idea of her size.

Looking around for a socket for her hairdryer, she was dismayed to find that although there were a few, none fitted her UK plug. Mildly put out, she towel dried it instead, before plaiting it into a thick braid. She would simply have to learn to adapt as best she could to her new environment. After all, she thought with some longing, she was unlikely to find all the conveniences of her home city several hours' drive into the African bush. Nevertheless, she thought with exasperation, there were some things she couldn't possibly be expected to do without, and a hairdryer was one of them!

Following the footpath that led from her cottage, she entered the rear of the hospital where most of the wards were situated on different sides of a long passageway. She stepped into the first room on her right through double swing doors and was greeted warmly by a smiling Sister Ngoba, the night sister whom she'd met the previous evening and who was now busy writing up reports before handing over to the day staff. As Kirsty's eyes roamed the length of the ward, she was surprised to see a familiar head bent over the bed of a female patient whose leg was in traction. When he looked up she could see the stubble darkening his jaw and the fatigue shadowing his eyes.

'Kirsty?' he said, sounding surprised. 'You don't need to be on duty until tomorrow. Everyone needs a day to settle in.'

'I know. I wanted to check up on how our patients from the accident yesterday were doing. And I'm longing to get started. I don't need a day off. Anyway, you're on duty,' she challenged.

He smiled tiredly. 'But I'm *meant* to be on duty.'

'You haven't been up all night, have you?'

'Almost, but not quite,' he said, wryly thinking that the hour's sleep he'd managed to get hadn't been nearly enough. 'Thank you for your help yesterday, by the way, and a belated welcome to the team. You'll meet everyone later.'

'I look forward to that.' She paused to smile hello at the patient Greg had been examining. It was the young woman whose tibia and fibula had been badly crushed by the overturned minibus. Lydia, her eyes cloudy with painkillers, managed a weak smile in return, before closing her eyes.

'How's our patient?' Kirsty asked quietly.

'I think we've managed to save her leg. Once I'm sure she's stable, I'll arrange to send her to one of the hospitals in the city. They have better equipment than we do, as well as access to physio. For cases like this we patch them up, stabilise them and then send them on.' He smiled down at the girl and said something to her that Kirsty couldn't understand.

'You speak the language?' Kirsty asked impressed.

'One or two of them—there are around fifteen different languages or dialects in this country, but I know the ones that are spoken in this neck of the woods. I find it's pretty useful for communicating with my patients.' He stretched, working the kinks out of his muscles. 'But obviously you'll need a nurse or an assistant to help you translate when there are patients who don't speak English.' Kirsty made a mental note to try and master as much of the language as she could. She had learned a few words before coming out, mainly greetings, but intended to learn more.

'I'm just telling Lydia that the morphine that we've given her is what's making her sleepy. She'll probably be out for the count for the rest of the day,' Greg explained, and sure enough Lydia had closed her eyes and seemed to have already succumbed to the sedating effects of the drug. Kirsty and Greg moved away from the bed.

'I also hoped for a tour of the rest of the hospital. I'm really keen to see it all.'

Greg wrapped his stethoscope around his neck. 'I could show you later,' he replied.

'Please, don't worry. I'm sure you've got enough to do. One of the nursing sisters can— or, if everyone's busy, I can see myself around. I won't get in anyone's way—I promise. But first I need a cup of coffee! I haven't had any yet and I'm a bit of a caffeine junkie.'

Greg hit his forehead with the heel of his hand. 'Damn, I'm sorry about that. I meant to organise some provisions for you yesterday but with everything going so crazy here, it completely slipped my mind.' His sheepish grin was contrite.

'I'm almost finished the ward rounds so if you can hold on, I'll show you the dining room. Then unfortunately I'm due in Outpatients so I'll have to leave you to your own devices.'

'I'll come with you to Outpatients, if that's OK. I'd really like to get stuck in as soon as possible. A coffee and toast will do me until lunch,' she said.

Greg looked at her appraisingly. Kirsty couldn't help notice how the corners of his eyes crinkled when he smiled. But even when relaxed there was a presence about the man, an animal-like energy that seemed to fill the room.

'We could do with the help. Jamie and Sarah are in Theatre this morning and Jenny is an-aesthetising for them, so quick rounds, followed by coffee and Outpatients it is.' He went on, 'This, as I'm sure you've gathered, is the female surgical ward.' He moved to the next bed. 'You recognise this young lady?'

It was the woman who had had the femoral bleed, Maria. A quick look at her chart told Kirsty that she was stable.

'I take it if she's not in Intensive Care, she's going to be all right?'

'We had her in surgery most of the night, but it looks hopeful. Once we're sure she can tolerate the journey, we'll send her by ambulance to one of the teaching hospitals in the city. They'll be able to take it from there.'

'And Lydia's little boy? Where is he?' asked Kirsty, suddenly remembering.

'He's in the paediatric ward for the time being. There was nowhere else to put him. He's been driving the staff crazy with his loud wailing. He won't be consoled. We'd let him see his mother if she looked a little less frightening. Can't you hear him?'

And Kirsty did, faintly. She found herself moving in the direction of his cries.

'Any relatives we can contact?'

'No one's come forward to claim him but it's early still. When the mother surfaces properly, we'll get more information.'

'I think he should see her,' she said firmly.

'Would that be wise?'

'He's, what…about two years old? Old enough for some understanding. I think he needs to *feel* his mother's still alive, even though she's "sleeping".'

'It might make things worse. Surely it's better to wait until she's alert enough to reassure him herself?' he suggested.

'How could anything be worse for him than what it is now? He's not crying just because he's miserable and wants to make a loud noise. He's crying for his mother, and he can't understand why she's not coming. In his mind she's abandoned him.'

'If you're sure…'

'I'm not sure. It depends on his ability to comprehend. But he seemed so well cared-for I'm willing to take a gamble… Besides, I do know a thing or two about children.' Kirsty felt the familiar crushing pain as she said the words. She ignored Greg's searching glance and turned towards the cries before he could say anything.

They entered the children's ward together. The toddler was not the only one crying but he was certainly the loudest. Kirsty's greeting of the staff on duty was cursory as she focused her attention on the unhappy child. Picking him up, she depended on the natural inherent curiosity of toddlers for him to be distracted long enough for her to talk to him. She was confident that, like most very young children, he understood a lot more than most adults would give him credit for. Recalling the desperate concern of the mother at the accident scene, this child knew love.

'Shh,' she said, soothing the distressed infant, dangling her stethoscope in front of him. It took a while but he quietened eventually as, momentarily distracted, he explored his new toy. Kirsty knew that it wouldn't be long before his cries resumed.

She caught sight of one of his fingers, which had a sticky plaster on it, a superficial pre-crash wound she'd noticed yesterday.

'Ow,' she said, lifting his hand and kissing the well-wrapped injury. The little boy seemed hypnotised by her attention. 'What's "Mother sleeping"?' she asked the staff while the boy gazed, astonished, at his finger, as if seeing it for the first time in a new light. 'Tell him his mummy has a big "ow" and is sleeping.' The nurse spoke to the child and he listened, taking in what was being said to him.

Armed with a few new words of the language, Kirsty followed Greg back to the surgical ward.

'Mummy's sleeping—*bomma robetsego,*' she tried in his language as the toddler stared down at his mother. His bottom lip quivered and Kirsty knew tears were not far behind. In an age-long gesture, he leaned out of Kirsty's arms, his arms stretched pleadingly towards his unconscious mother.

'Mummy's sleeping. Shh,' Kirsty repeated softly, allowing him to touch the still figure. 'Let her sleep.'

The little boy crumpled in her arms. This time, though, his tears were quieter as she took him away and returned him to the children's ward.

'Well, I'll be damned!' Greg said, walking alongside her.

'It doesn't always work,' Kirsty admitted, 'but I thought it worth a try. He's exhausted so hopefully he'll sleep now, and when he wakes up someone should take him back to see his mother. With a bit of luck she'll wake soon and comfort him herself.'

'And if she doesn't?'

'Then he'll know why,' she replied simply. 'If not now, then later when it matters.

Children are more able to cope with a parent who can't help or comfort them. It's those who think their parents have abandoned them who suffer most.'

Greg flinched and he looked off into the distance, before striding out of the ward, leaving Kirsty to scurry along in his wake. It seemed she had touched a nerve. She was dismayed and not a little curious. What on earth had she said that had affected him like that?

In the male surgical ward, Dr Jenny Carter was taking a blood sample from a patient. She looked up as she heard the ward doors swing open.

Kirsty found her instantly likeable. Plump, with a thick bush of greying hair tied back at the nape of her neck with what looked like a shoelace, she had a gregarious, warm manner.

'Ah, our new recruit! Come to check we're taking good care of your patients from last night?' But there wasn't an ounce of malice in the question. 'Here's Mr Mhlongo. Says we can call him Eddy! And he must be doing fine because he's already been teasing the nurses. Perhaps we should plaster the other arm, what do you think?' A nursing sister cheerfully translated the doctor's words to Eddy.

'*Dumela,*' Kirsty greeted the chuckling man, covered in plaster on one side of his chest all the way down to his fingers with his neck stabilised in a brace. He might not have realised it yet but he owed his life to the seat belt that had prevented him from meeting a similar fate to the driver when the front of the minibus had slammed into the ground. She felt his pulse and although she'd been concerned he might have sustained a serious concussion, his bright eyes told her otherwise. A broken shoulder and a severe case of whiplash seemed to be the worst of his problems. Not so the patient in the bed closest to the nurses' station or the one in Intensive Care, but the two other patients in the ward she'd attended to yesterday were doing fine.

Kirsty was surprised at the number of patients in the hospital cared for by a very small complement of staff. In fact, some wards were so crowded that some patients were sleeping on mattresses on the floor or, as the case in the children's ward, doubled up in cots.

'What about the risk of cross-infection?' she asked Greg.

'We are as careful as we can be. Most of those sharing are siblings with the same condition.'

'Surely not those with HIV or AIDS?'

'Actually, contrary to popular belief, it is these patients who need to be protected from infection and not the other way around. After all, it is their immune systems that are compromised, rendering them vulnerable to every infection and germ around,' Greg told Kirsty. He turned to the nursing sister who was accompanying them. 'Isn't that right, Sister?'

The nursing sister shrugged her shoulders. 'Too many with the disease. We try to take special care but...' The shake of her head told much without words. It had been a fact of life for so long that it was difficult, if not impossible, not to become desensitised.

'Come on, let's get you fed and then, if you're still up for it, you can come and help me in Outpatients. Although it's Sunday, we'll have a full clinic. Days of the week have no meaning out here. Most of them will have walked for days just to get here and I don't like to keep them waiting any longer than necessary. I've eaten...' he glanced at his watch '...but I've time for a quick cup of coffee, so I'll show you where the staff dining room is then leave you to it. The other staff will probably be there, except for the Campbells who tend to eat breakfast in their own house.'

When they entered the dining room she was pleased to find Jenny there if no one else.

'Jenny will show you to Outpatients when you're ready. Take your time,' Greg said, and after a quick gulp of coffee left the two women to it.

'Does he ever slow down?' Kirsty asked, looking at Greg's retreating back.

'Not really,' Jenny acknowledged. 'The man is a human dynamo. I can't remember the last time he took a day off. The rest of us are more human: he insists we take a couple of days at least every third week.' She eyed Kirsty's thin frame thoughtfully. 'Don't worry, no one will expect you to work these hours, dear.'

'I'll do my share,' Kirsty said. 'I'm stronger than I look.' She stirred the lumpy porridge thoughtfully. 'Maybe Greg works too hard,' she said, choosing her words carefully. 'Sometimes he seems a little...well, abrupt. Or is it just me? Have I done something wrong?'

'Oh, don't mind Greg. His bark is worse than his bite. He's a real softy really. As you'll find out.'

'Softy' was the last word Kirsty would have used to describe Greg. 'What happened to him?' she asked, curious to know more about this man she was to work with over the coming months.

'You mean his face? The scars? I hardly notice them any more.' Jenny hesitated for a moment before seeming to make up her mind. 'Oh, well, you'll find out sooner rather than later anyway. It's impossible to keep secrets in a community of this size. He got them trying to rescue his wife and child from their burning house. They were on their own, just before Christmas—five years last Christmas, in fact. He had been called to the hospital—some emergency I expect. He arrived home to find his house in flames and the fire brigade battling to get it under control. His wife and daughter were still inside. Greg tried to get to them even though the firemen had already failed. They couldn't hold him back. He went in and brought them out. But it was too late. They had both died from smoke inhalation. Apparently the fire started from the Christmas-tree lights. He was devastated. They were his whole world. I don't think he has ever come to terms with the loss—I'm not sure that one does.'

Kirsty was stricken. Memories of her own tragedy came flooding back. Although fifteen years had passed, there wasn't a day when she didn't think of her mother or Pamela.

Jenny shook her head sorrowfully, unaware of Kirsty's reaction. 'I think Greg blames himself, God knows why. There wasn't anything anybody could have done. The poor man was in hospital himself for weeks. Once he was discharged he left Cape Town. I expect he couldn't bear to stay anywhere near the place where they had been so happy. He came here and has been here ever since. He works so hard. It's as if he is trying to exorcise his demons through sheer hard work. He never talks about it or them, and if I were you, I wouldn't ever raise the topic. I tried once and got my head bitten off.'

'How awful.' Kirsty blinked away the tears that

threatened to surface. No wonder he was brusque. Now she knew, she would have to be more sympathetic.

'He still wears his wedding ring,' she said.

'You noticed, then?' Jenny cast a mischievous look at Kirsty. 'I wouldn't get any ideas in that direction. There has been many a young doctor and nurse who has tried to offer Greg comfort, but while he doesn't seem adverse to the odd casual fling, I doubt somehow that he'll ever let anyone really get under the barrier of ice he seems to have wrapped around his heart.'

Kirsty felt her cheeks flame at the implication. 'I can assure you,' she said stiffly, 'a relationship with anyone is the last thing on my mind.'

Subconsciously she fingered her now bare ring finger. 'I've had enough of men to last me a lifetime.' She ignored Jenny's curious look. 'I'm here to work and to learn. Nothing more.' She drained her coffee. 'Sorry.' Kirsty grimaced, suddenly aghast at the turn the conversation had taken. The kindly doctor in front of her must think her rude. 'I'm not usually so prickly, it's just…new place, new people, new challenges. It'll take me a day or two to settle in, I guess.'

By the time Jenny left Kirsty outside the outpatient clinic, with a hasty apology that she had another Theatre list due to start, there were several patients sitting outside, waiting their turn to be seen. Most of the women still wore traditional dress and despite the intense heat had their children strapped onto their backs with thick blankets. For the most part the children seemed quiet—subdued even. One little boy squatted in the dust, lazily poking at the ground with a stick. When he looked up Kirsty could see that one of his eyes was sticky with what looked like a chronic infection. She tilted his chin—he needed something for his eyes, the sooner the better. She glanced around and spotted a nurse moving between the patients, taking histories and writing notes. Kirsty guessed she was probably assessing who needed to be seen first. Just before Kirsty could grab her attention she noticed a young woman clutching a bundle to her breast. There was something in the woman's posture—an air of despair—that made Kirsty catch her breath. She moved closer, and gently lowered the blanket to reveal a small, painfully thin child who was making no effort to take the proffered breast of the young mother. The child's face was so thin it seemed almost skeletal, the skin clinging to the fragile bones of the skull. Flies settled and buzzed around the tiny mouth and closed eyes. For a heart-stopping moment Kirsty thought the child was already dead. She felt for a pulse and was rewarded with a faint flutter beneath her fingertips. The child was still alive, but surely not for long. With one swift movement she lifted the infant up, its tiny frame feeling no heavier than a feather, and rushed into the department. This child couldn't wait. It needed fluids in the form of a drip straight away or he or she would die.

Ignoring the wails of the young mother, she searched frantically for Greg. She found him crouching in front of an old woman, examining a suppurating sore on her foot.

Greg took one look at Kirsty's anguished expression and stood up.

'What is it?' he asked, bending forward to look

at her small bundle. 'Not another case of marasmus—starvation,' he said despairingly. 'OK, bring her into the treatment room and let's see what we can do. If there is anything we can do.'

Within moments the small child, a girl, was lying on the couch, her mother sitting close by, her eyes flitting from Kirsty to Greg. One of the nurses had joined them and was talking to the mother in rapid Sotho.

'The child stopped taking the breast two days ago. She's been sick for over a week. A traditional healer gave her mother some herbs to give her, but when they didn't help and she stopped taking the breast, the mother decided to bring her to us. It's taken two days for her to get here.'

While the nurse repeated the history, Greg and Kirsty had been searching for a vein in which to insert a drip. Kirsty knew that they had to get the small child rehydrated as soon as possible.

'I can't find any in her arms. They all seem to have collapsed,' Kirsty told Greg, fear catching her voice. They had no time. The child could die if they didn't treat her right away.

Greg looked up at her. 'Slow down. We'll find

one. Look here just above the foot. We'll need to do a cut down. It's not ideal, but it's all we have. Have you done one before?'

'I have, but I'd rather watch you first, if that's OK,' Kirsty said. This child was so small, so desperately ill. What if she was too slow?

'You'll have to do it, I'm afraid. You may have noticed my right hand only has restricted movement. It's fine except for the most delicate stuff.' Kirsty could only guess what it cost Greg to admit his limitations. At the same time she admired him for it. She had once seen a doctor attempt to perform procedures above his capabilities and the results had almost been disastrous.

Greg noticed Kirsty's hesitation. 'You'll be fine. I'll talk you through it.'

Somehow his belief in her gave her confidence and with very little assistance from Greg she performed the procedure perfectly and without any wasted time.

'Excellent job.' Greg's praise was fulsome and genuine and Kirsty felt elated. She thought that she might grow to like her job here.

'OK, let's get her started on the usual regime.' He directed a few rapid words towards the mother.

'She's three years old,' he translated for Kirsty.

Once again Kirsty was horrified. Three! It wasn't possible. The child looked no older than nine months, a year at the most. She was so tiny.

'Obviously we can't use her age to work out how much we need to give her. By my guess she weighs just over eight kilograms. Could you pop her on the scales?' he asked the nurse.

The nurse scooped the child up and laid her gently on the scales.

'Just right—eight kilos,' she told Greg.

'Any thoughts on the dosage we should be administering?' Greg asked Kirsty.

Kirsty thought frantically. She had completed six months in paediatrics as part of her houseman jobs. But the children there had been so much bigger, stronger than this child in front of her. She had never seen anyone in such an advanced stage of starvation before. How could she have? But she remembered a child, physically handicapped, who had been brought in following a severe episode of diarrhoea. The child's condition had been similar to if not quite as drastic as that of this child in front of her.

She was about to hazard a guess, but Greg hadn't waited for her response. He adjusted the drip and straightened up. She could sense the fatigue and something else—could it be anger?—behind his professional exterior.

'We've done everything we can for the time being. It's in the lap of the gods now.' He tossed his gloves into the bin. 'The main problem is caused by formula. The government spends sub-stantial sums of money promoting breast-feeding, but the problem is with the women who are HIV positive. The danger of them transmitting the disease to their infants through breast milk is just too large, so they are encouraged to give their babies formula. Unfortunately formula is too ex-pensive for most of them, so they start diluting it to make it go further. Then the children simply don't get enough calories or nutrition. And as if that isn't bad enough, a large number of the outlying villages still don't have access to clean water. So the women mix the powder with water from the river. And what you see before you is the result.'

'Can't we do anything about it?' Kirsty asked. 'Surely it's just a matter of education?'

Greg smiled, but there was no humour in his eyes. 'Education and clean water. That's what is needed. In the meantime…' He let the words hang in the air for a moment. 'In the meantime we do the best we can. Come on, Kirsty, as you're about to see, there is plenty more for us to do.'

'But doing the best we can isn't *enough*. Is it? Not if children are still dying?' Surely he wasn't going to tell her there was nothing they could do to prevent this? He didn't strike Kirsty as a man who let anything stop him from doing what was right.

'We'll talk about it later,' Greg said quietly but firmly. 'Right now we have work to do. You take the consulting room next door. I'm just across the hall. If you need me, give me a shout, but try the nurses first. I think you'll find that there is precious little they can't help you with.' And without waiting for a reply, he turned on his heel and left the room.

CHAPTER THREE

THE rest of the morning passed quickly. Kirsty saw many children with the swollen bellies and stick-like limbs of kwashiorkor, a condition the nurses told her was caused by poor nutrition and lack of vitamins. The nursing staff were fantastic. They worked unstintingly throughout the day, pausing to answer Kirsty's questions with unfailing good humour and patience. Kirsty felt humbled to be part of their team and full of admiration for their level of expertise. The patients too were remarkably stoic and, despite long waits in the overcrowded department, were universally grateful for everything Kirsty did, however small. Occasionally, to her surprise, she could hear laughter filtering through the walls of the consulting room.

Eventually the clinic quietened down, until all

that was left was dressings and vaccinations that the nursing staff on the back shift would finish off.

As Kirsty leaned back in her chair, a wave of exhaustion washed over her. But it felt good. She closed her eyes.

'Lunch?' Greg popped his head around the door and as if in answer Kirsty's stomach growled. Now that he mentioned it, she was starving. The cup of coffee and the watery porridge she had eaten at breakfast-time had made her appreciate why the others ate at home. As soon as she had the opportunity she was going to stock up on provisions, but in the meantime…

'Lead me to it,' she said, jumping out of her chair. *I hope he doesn't think I've spent the morning snoozing,* she thought.

'Come on, then. I gather you did pretty well this morning. The nurse told me you worked throughout without a break. Well done.'

Kirsty felt herself glow with pleasure. Maybe he wasn't going to be so difficult to work for after all.

'I am going out to one of the villages tomorrow to do a clinic, if you'd like to come with me,' Greg said as they made their way to the staff dining room. Kirsty almost had to run to keep up with his long strides. 'You've seen the bad, now I'd like you to see the good.'

'I'd love to,' Kirsty said, 'but I'd like to check up on the child we saw this morning before lunch, if that's OK. I don't mind missing lunch if we're pushed for time.'

Greg's eyes swept over her figure. He shook his head. 'You look as if you could do with a good feeding up yourself, so missing lunch isn't a good idea. You've been working hard and a sick or weakened doctor is no good to anyone. Of course we can take the time to pop into Paediatrics before we eat, but if you are going to survive out here, you'll need to become less emotionally involved. I find too much emotion can cloud a doctor's judgement.'

So much for thinking he was going to be easy to work for! It hadn't taken long for his habitual curtness to resurface. And who was he to tell her when she had to eat? And as for telling her not to become too involved, she had heard those words before. She thought it would be different out here. She thought, if anything, doctors came here to work because they wanted to be involved. But clearly not Dr Greg du Toit. The man had no feelings. He was simply a working machine.

'I think I'm old enough to look after myself,' Kirsty said frostily. 'I don't mind you commenting on my work, but what I eat and what I feel is up to me, don't you think?'

Her words stopped Greg in his tracks. He turned to look at Kirsty with glittering blue eyes. Suddenly he smiled.

'OK, OK.' He put his hands up in mock surrender. 'You win. However, no missing meals—is that understood?'

'Yeah, yeah, and no late nights or alcohol or strange men in my room after midnight. Gotcha.'

Greg's smile grew broader. 'God, I do sound like a Victorian father, don't I? Kathleen was always telling me to lighten up.' His smile disappeared and Kirsty could see the pain in his eyes. For a moment she was tempted to reach out to offer him comfort. She touched his arm gently, feeling the muscles tense beneath her fingertips.

'Was Kathleen your wife?' she asked softly.

He drew back from her touch as if she'd caused him physical pain.

'Ah, I see people have been talking,' he said, his lips set in a grim line.

'Jenny told me what happened. I'm so sorry, Greg. I don't know how anyone can bear such a loss.'

'Well, let's hope you never have to find out,' he said, rubbing his hand across his scars. 'Some things are just better not thought about.'

That's where you are wrong, thought Kirsty, feeling the familiar flicker of pain.

'You must miss them,' Kirsty ventured. Inexplicably she felt the need to get closer to this man.

'As you told me just a few minutes ago, everyone has a right to their privacy. I've agreed to respect yours and I'd be grateful if you would respect mine.' Despite his words, his tone was mild. But Kirsty could see by the set of his jaw that he was holding himself in check.

Nevertheless, Kirsty felt as if she'd been slapped.

'I'm sorry,' she said stiffly. 'I didn't mean to pry.'

Greg rubbed his scar. 'No, forgive me,' he said.

'I didn't mean to have a go at you. I've probably been here too long and have forgotten the social niceties. Let's just forget it.'

He paused next to a path that led away from the hospital towards the perimeter of the compound. 'If you follow that path for a few minutes, you'll come to a large concrete reservoir. We use it for swimming. Jamie makes it his business to keep it clean. We often congregate there after work or at weekends.' He carried on walking. 'There are four doctors here, as you know—you make the fifth. We take turns at being on call, and we all operate but Sarah is nominally in charge of obstetrics, Jamie paediatrics, Jenny anaesthetises and has responsibility for the medical wards. The surgical wards are mine. There's a rota for outpatients as that involves a bit of everything.'

'What will I be doing?' Kirsty asked

'You'll be learning.' He looked at her intently. 'At this point you have no idea how quickly you'll be learning. A couple of weeks and you'll be expected to manage on your own, although, of course, we will always be available for advice.

I'm afraid, Dr Boucher, we can't carry people here. It's a case of see one, do one, teach one.'

There was no mistaking his meaning. If she didn't live up to his expectations, she'd be on the next plane home. For a moment she felt a flutter of anxiety. She was a good doctor, she knew that—but it was all so different here.

He stopped outside the staff house. 'Come on, let's get you fed.' He grinned as he caught her warning look, his smile making him look younger and carefree, and for a moment Kirsty could see a different side to her boss. 'And introduce you to the rest of the team, of course.'

There were five or six people seated at the table. Jenny smiled a greeting and Greg introduced a striking-looking couple as Sarah and Jamie, the doctors Campbell. There were two men who were introduced to Kirsty as outreach workers. 'Thandi and Johan spend their time sinking wells in the outlying villages. We'll be going to one of them tomorrow. Clean water is one of the things that really makes a difference to the health of the villagers.'

There was also Sibongele, a young man with

chocolate skin and deep brown eyes. Sibongele stood and, grabbing a couple of roast potatoes, headed towards the door.

'Pleased to meet you, Dr Boucher,' he said in faultless English, 'but if you'll excuse me, I'm due in Theatre.'

Catching Kirsty's look of confusion, Sarah explained. 'Sibongele is our foster-son. He helps out as a Theatre orderly when he's not at school. He plans to study medicine when he finishes high school. All his spare time, apart from the odd game of football, is spent hanging about the hospital.'

'I thought he looked a bit young—even to be a medical student.' Kirsty admitted.

Sarah laughed. 'Believe me, Sibongele is twice as good as some of the medical students we've had.'

Kirsty was drawn to Sarah, with her open smile and sparkling eyes. Her husband Jamie stood and pulled out a chair for Kirsty. 'Welcome, Kirsty. You've no idea how badly we need an extra pair of hands.'

'I think she's probably got the picture, Jamie,' Greg said, passing Kirsty a bowl of sweet potatoes. 'She's seen for herself how busy we are. She worked like a Trojan this morning.'

Kirsty felt herself flush at his praise. She knew that he was being kind. All the clinical staff were so much more experienced than her. She was terrified she'd end up being more of a hindrance than a help.

'Don't worry, Kirsty, if you find it all a bit overwhelming,' Sarah said. 'I did at first. It's all so different to being in a properly equipped and orderly A and E department. But when you get used to it, there is nothing like it. You really feel that here you can make a difference.'

Before Kirsty had a chance to reply, all eyes turned towards the door. A gleeful toddler rushed into the room, followed by a clucking woman. 'Hey, Calum, you're too fast for Koko now. Leave Mummy to finish eating.'

'It's all right, Martha,' Sarah said, scooping the chuckling toddler into her arms. 'I've finished and I need a cuddle with this young man,' she added, tickling the delighted boy. 'Kirsty, this is our son, Calum.'

'Your son?' Kirsty echoed 'You brought your

son here? Aren't you worried about bringing him up here? So far away from civilisation. And exposed to so much disease.' The words had slipped out before she could prevent them. For a moment there was a deathly silence. Sarah's smile froze and Jamie narrowed his eyes.

'Mmm. Civilisation—whatever that is. But I can't say I feel Calum is deprived. We've been here about six months and, as you can see, he's thriving,' Sarah said. 'He has plenty of attention and there are lots of other children he can play with. And as for disease—obviously he has been vaccinated. Naturally, we don't let him near any of the contagious patients,' she finished softly.

The smile returned as she turned to her husband. 'I did worry about bringing him out here at first— of course, any mother would—but I knew Jamie would never expose his child to danger.'

The look that passed between Sarah and Jamie was affectionate. It was obvious they were very much in love. 'We would never risk anything happening to our child. We almost lost him once, so would never do anything that would put him at risk, believe me.'

'I'm sorry…I didn't mean to imply… You must think me so rude. Of course you would never put your son in harm's way. I'm such an idiot. Sometimes I open my mouth without engaging my brain. You're obviously not the kind of parents that would put their child in danger.' As soon as the words were out of her mouth Kirsty could have bitten her tongue. She glanced over at Greg just in time to see him flinch. How could she have been so insensitive? She should just shut up instead of making matters worse! 'Oh, dear…' she began.

The sound of a chair being scraped back stopped Kirsty in mid-flow. Greg tossed his napkin onto the table, his face pale and his mouth set in a grim line.

'I've had enough,' he said quietly. 'I'm going back to my house. Jamie, perhaps you could take Kirsty around the wards with you this afternoon?' His gaze swung to her, his eyes cool. 'Or, since this is meant to be a day off for you, maybe you'd prefer to go to the shops with Sarah? I'm afraid that's as close to civilisation as we can offer you. You might even find one or two clothes shops.'

'I didn't mean...' Kirsty felt herself go pink. No matter what, she seemed to say the wrong thing in front of Greg. She felt a stab of disappointment as his cool eyes flicked over her. Was that what he really thought of her? A shallow city girl obsessed with shopping? She stifled the words of protest that sprang to her lips. She'd already said too much. She took a deep breath. 'Of course I'll need to go shopping at some time, but only to stock up on food. I could give you a list, Sarah, if that's OK with you? Then I could stay and do rounds with Jamie.'

'Whatever,' Greg said. 'See the rest of you at dinner.' He left the room, leaving an embarrassed silence in his wake.

'Don't worry, Kirsty,' Sarah said, noticing her distress. 'Try not to take it personally. You hit a sore spot. But he's really a lamb under that tough exterior.' Sarah ignored her husband's snort of disbelief. 'It's just that we've been let down badly by doctors in the past. They come out here, looking for God knows what, and then within a couple of weeks they find it's too remote and too basic so they just leave. Then we have wasted our time training people who don't stay. But I'm sure you're going to be different. What brings you here anyway? You were a last-minute substitution for someone else, weren't you?'

Kirsty thought rapidly. She couldn't possibly tell them the truth now. If they knew why she'd come here, they'd believe their worse suspicions confirmed. And suddenly Kirsty couldn't bear them to think less of her. Perhaps when she had accepted the job at short notice it had been for the wrong reasons. In that she was no better than the doctors Sarah had talked about. And, yes, she had been horrified—was still horrified—at how basic and isolated the hospital was. She was a city girl used to first-class medical amenities after all. There was nothing wrong with liking clubs and theatres and shopping, was there? You could still like all that and be a good doctor, couldn't you? But now she had made the commitment to the hospital, she intended to stay and play her part. She had no intention, no matter how tough and no matter how disagreeable her boss was, of leaving. All she really worried about at this stage was whether she could cope. Not just with the work, but the lifestyle, the bugs. She shivered, remembering the large insect that had scuttled across her foot that morning.

'Er, I had just finished a stint at A and E and I had taken six months off to travel across Australia with a friend. But that fell through at the last minute.' It wasn't exactly a lie, Kirsty thought, mentally crossing her fingers. 'Then a work colleague mentioned this place and that you were desperate for doctors. So it seemed perfect,' she finished triumphantly.

'Well, we are glad to have you,' Sarah said. 'I only work part time so I can spend time with Calum. I usually end up doing the shopping trips. And, of course, I'm happy to take your list. When you do have some time off, we can go together, if you like. I for one miss the occasional trips to civilisation, and another female for company.' She winked at Kirsty.

Jamie stood up. 'If you two have finished, we'd better get on. Ready, Kirsty?'

Kirsty unwound her stethoscope from around her neck and lifted her hair off her collar to ease the tension in her neck. Her skin felt clammy and she longed for a breeze to cool her overheated body. The last few hours on the wards had been so busy she hadn't had time to notice how inadequate the air-conditioning was in the hospital building but now she was aware her clothes were sticking to her. Waving a tired goodbye to the nursing staff, she remembered the pool that Greg had mentioned. A swim would be ideal right now. Incredible that even with the sun so low in the sky, it should be so hot and humid still.

Finding the path again, she turned down it, enjoying the shade cast by a magnificent jacaranda tree and a fence listing under the weight of bougainvillea. The circular reservoir was virtually hidden by the lush growth of honeysuckle and other shrubs surrounding its high walls. Wondering if the water would be clean enough to swim in, she climbed the ladder at the side until she was standing on top of the broad wall. The water was clear, blue and extremely inviting. The thought of it on her skin was too tempting for Kirsty to resist. Glancing around to check there was no one about, she stripped off her scrubs and stood in her underwear. She hesitated only a moment before taking a deep breath and lowering herself gingerly into the water. She gasped as found herself submerged in the icy water. Despite the initial shock, it felt wonderful after the searing heat.

She swam a few lengths before turning on her back and letting herself float. She gazed up at the cloudless sky and let her mind wander. It had been an eventful day. She hadn't really thought about what she would face when she had got here. She had been too desperate to put as much distance as possible between her and Robbie. Kirsty knew she would have gone to the moon if it had been the only place left to get away to. But now she was glad that she had ended up here. Already she felt drawn into this world and cared about the people who depended so desperately on this team of highly skilled and dedicated doctors and nurses.

A shadow fell across her face. Opening her eyes, she squinted into the sun to find Greg's tall figure standing looking down at her. He was dressed only in a pair of Bermuda shorts and was holding a towel in his hand. His chest was bronzed and muscular and Kirsty was disconcertedly aware of the dark hair on his lean abdomen. Her eyes travelled back upwards, her breath catching in her throat as she saw the scars that marred his chest and shoulder. She forced her eyes away and found his eyes, which seemed to glitter in the dying light.

'I'm sorry,' he said,' I didn't realise that anyone was using the pool. I'll leave you in peace to enjoy your swim.' Something in his expression made her suddenly conscious that she was only wearing her underwear and, glancing down, she was horrified to realise that it had become transparent. Quickly she began to tread water, trying to hide herself beneath the swirling water.

'Don't go,' she said. 'There's room enough here for both of us. Besides, I was planning to get out soon.' She turned away and started swimming, hoping to hide her confusion in action.

She felt a splash as Greg dived into the water. She rested for a while and watched his swift, sure strokes as he swam to and fro. Clearly he was an experienced swimmer. She wasn't a bad swimmer herself, but she was slightly out of breath after a couple of minutes. He surfaced beside her, shaking the water from his thick hair. She could make out the faint crinkles around his eyes. Excruciatingly aware of his nearly naked body next to hers, separated only by a couple of inches of water, she felt a tingle of desire low in her abdomen. What was wrong with her? She was still in love with Robbie, wasn't she? She couldn't possibly be lusting after another man. Maybe it was her dented ego, wanting to check out whether she was still desirable. Perhaps an affair, no strings attached, was just what she needed. But if it was, her libido had chosen the wrong man. She couldn't imagine Greg being interested in any woman, least of all *her*. Catching Greg looking at her speculatively, she prayed the man couldn't read her mind.

'I think I'll get out,' she said, needing to get away from the confused thoughts his proximity was generating.

'OK,' Greg said, before plunging back into the water.

She turned to get out, only to discover that the

water level was too low for her to grab the side of the reservoir and pull herself out. She looked around for a ladder and realised there wasn't one on the inside.

She made a couple of attempts to heave herself over the side before conceding failure. She just didn't have the upper body strength necessary to do it.

How mortifying, she thought as she realised she was going to have to ask for assistance. It was either that or spend the night in the pool. Little as she liked having to ask for Greg's help, it was marginally more appealing than passing the night in a watery bed. She turned around to find him watching her, a grin playing on his lips as he trod water.

'Can't manage?' he said. 'I thought you city girls were all into the gym.'

'This city girl has been too busy with work—*and other things*,' she added under her breath, 'to go to the gym. So if you wouldn't mind helping me?'

Greg narrowed his eyes at her as if the thought of leaving her had also entered his mind, then with a fluid bunching of muscles he hauled himself out of the pool and came to stand in front of her.

'Take my hands,' he ordered.

Kirsty felt her hands grasped in his and as if she weighed nothing at all he pulled her out of the pool. The speed of her removal made her stumble against him and they both stepped back as Greg put his arms around her to steady her. She felt the cool heat of his skin against hers and the strength of his arms as he held her. Once more desire hit her like a tidal wave. Through the thin fabric of her underwear she could feel his answering response.

His hands moved over her shoulders, sweeping down to the small of her back. For a second she thought he was going to pull her closer but then he put her away from him.

'I told you, you don't eat enough. God, you hardly weigh more than a child.'

She felt his eyes rake her body, taking in her frame. His eyes paused on her breasts before slowly dropping downwards. She thought she heard him groan, before he cursed and bent to pick up his towel.

'Here, take this.'

Once again she was aware of her scanty attire. Heavens, she was practically naked in front of this man! She took the towel from him and wrapped it around her body. The sun was sinking in the sky, shooting ribbons of purple and pink, silhouetting the stark outlines of the acacia trees. The sound of rising starlings filled the air. Kirsty was bewitched. Africa was beginning to weave its magic.

'We'd better go,' Greg said brusquely. He turned his back and whipped off his wet shorts. Kirsty could just make out the lean contours of his naked buttocks before he pulled on his scrubs.

'Don't worry, I won't look if you want to do the same.'

'It's OK. I'll just get dressed over my wet clothes. I don't have far to go. My underwear will probably dry out in a minute.' She was aware that she was babbling but she felt confused by what had just happened. And what had that been? Nothing. He had helped her out of the pool—that was all. He had responded to her half-naked body like any other red-blooded male would have. But she suspected there was more to it than that. She was attracted to this man, despite being still in love with Robbie. It was crazy—she wasn't sure she even liked Greg du Toit. There was something too masculine, almost old-fashioned about him. And she was a thoroughly modern woman. She liked her men to be firmly part of the twenty-first century.

'By the way, your suitcases have arrived. What on earth have you brought? There seems to be at least four of them. Are you planning to stay here indefinitely?' Greg's voice broke into her thoughts.

Once more Kirsty felt defensive. 'It's probably my medical books. I thought they'd come in handy.' She winced inside at another white lie. OK, obviously there wasn't going to be an opportunity to wear all six of her party dresses, and perhaps she didn't need to bring quite as many pairs of shoes—but, bush or no bush, a girl still had to come prepared for any eventuality, didn't she?

'You must show me what you've brought,' Greg said with a sideways glance. 'We're always looking to update our skills with modern thinking—with all that literature, you're bound to be able to teach us a thing or two.'

Kirsty was aghast. But then, glancing up at him, she noticed a wicked twinkle in his eyes. Could he be teasing her?

Thankfully, before she could dig an even deeper hole for herself, he turned on his heel and, whistling, left her standing in the gathering dusk.

CHAPTER FOUR

DINNER that evening was a relaxed affair. As it was Kirsty's first proper evening everyone had turned up for the meal at staff house to welcome her. The dining room was bubbling with medical chat as everyone filled each other in with the day's events. Kirsty was relieved to note that all the staff sought opinions from each other. It seemed that sharing and discussing cases was the norm. Nobody seemed to hesitate to ask for advice.

'It's impossible for us all to know everything, and even what we do know counts for little out here where we have basic facilities.' Greg had turned to Kirsty after a particularly heated, though friendly debate with Sarah about a case. 'We often have to make different decisions out here than we would in a fully equipped hospital. Here we have to be aware of our limitations and the environment our patients are living in. For example, there is little point in asking someone to attend as an outpatient if they have to walk ten miles each way every day. Similarly we have to make decisions about performing surgery here versus waiting until the patient can be transferred to a major hospital, bearing in mind the trip takes several hours. Sometimes it's better not to give a C-section to a woman in labour—even when it seems on the face of it that it's clinically indicated.'

'But surely we have to do everything to ensure the survival of children or those who haven't been born? Isn't it fortunate that the patients end up here where we can section them and where we have at least basic facilities to support the neonates?'

'Well, yes and no,' said Greg, appearing to choose his words with care. He was leaning forward, elbows propped on his knees, his blue eyes holding Kirsty's with an almost magnetic pull. 'In the hospital, the child will have a reasonable chance of survival, but after that? You know that many neonates require intensive nursing for many months. We can't offer that here. They will have access to that kind of care if they can make it to the city. Not many do.'

Kirsty still couldn't quite believe what she was hearing.

'You can't possibly be suggesting we do nothing in these circumstances. It's our job, for God's sake. I for one could never stand back when I could help. And you can't ask me to.'

'No one is suggesting you do nothing. What I am suggesting is that we put the mother's life first—think of the implications surgery might have on her. What if she has one C-section, but then in subsequent pregnancies doesn't make it to the hospital in time, and her uterus ruptures and she dies? What of her unborn child then? More importantly, what of the children she has already? This country has been decimated by AIDS. There are already too many orphans even for the extended families to cope with.'

Kirsty sank back in her chair. Although instinctively she hated and rejected everything Greg was saying, she tried to see it from his point of view. But she couldn't. She hadn't become a doctor to stand back when she could help. But she remembered her father's words with a shiver—*You become too emotionally attached, Kirsty*—and he hadn't been the only person to say these words to her. She looked around at her colleagues. Why wasn't anyone arguing with him? Was this what happened when you worked in places like this? You became immune? You stopped thinking with your heart?

'So we just stand back,' Kirsty said, 'and do nothing.'

'We do what we can, Kirsty, but…' Greg stood, implying that as far as he was concerned the conversation was at a close. 'Whatever we do, we do it because it is best for our patients. Not because it's best for us. Now you are here, remember always to ask yourself the question, "Am I treating this patient because it will make the patient better or because it will make me feel better?"'

Kirsty opened her mouth to argue with him. Even if everyone else seemed to accept everything he said as gospel truth, she saw no reason why she should. *Except he has more experience than you,* the rational voice in her head argued, *years more experience. But*, the other more persistent voice argued back, *he's emotionally distant. Whatever happened to him in the past has removed his ability to care. And that can't be right either.* Before Kirsty could find the words to argue with him, Greg put his empty wineglass down and headed towards the door.

'If you'll excuse me. I had an early start this morning and I have another one tomorrow. Remember you're coming to the one of the clinics with me tomorrow, Kirsty. We leave at 6 a.m. sharp.' And then, with a goodbye to the others in the room, he was gone.

Kirsty turned to Sarah, who was gathering up Calum's belongings.

'Do you agree with him? You can't possibly believe that we should ever stand back and not use our medical skills whenever we can. That we act like we are gods, deciding who we should help and when.'

'I don't think that's what he meant at all, Kirsty,' Sarah said quietly, rising to her feet and passing her sleeping child to Jamie. 'Once you get to know Greg you'll know he always acts in the best interests of his patients. No matter how difficult that can be.

'What he's trying to say is that every day we face difficult choices here. Choices we never thought we'd have to make. Sometimes we have to make decisions that go against everything we have learned up until now. That's why we discuss cases with each other, ask each other for an opinion, a point of view. Nobody, least of all Greg, is asking you to make those kinds of decisions alone. Not until you've gained enough experience and confidence, and that will take time. A week or two, at any rate.' She smiled and Kirsty hoped that it meant she was joking.

'Don't tease her, SJ,' Jamie admonished gently, winking at Kirsty. 'We'll be here to help and advise you for a lot longer than a couple of weeks. Greg and I have both spent a long time working in these conditions and we still run situations past each other—there is no shame in that. Where doctors do get themselves into difficulty is when they don't seek advice, but I'm sure you aren't that kind of doctor.' Jamie cocked an eyebrow in her direction.

For a second Kirsty felt flustered. What was he implying? But then, just as quickly, the moment passed. There was no malice in either Sarah or her husband. It was simply that she was feeling overly sensitive. All of a sudden a wave of fatigue engulfed her. Although it wasn't quite ten in the evening, she was exhausted. Normally at this time she'd be getting ready to go to some club with Robbie or some of her friends. Here, however, all she wanted to do was crawl into bed and drag the covers over her head.

'I guess it's another thing I have to adapt to in Africa,' Kirsty replied, with a self-conscious smile. 'And I certainly hope I never become the kind of doctor that feels above asking a colleague for advice or an opinion.'

Sarah nodded. 'There's a lot to take in when you come here, but I can tell you're going to fit in just fine.'

Kirsty stifled a yawn as she said goodnight to everyone. It had been an interesting evening, she mused as she made her way back to her rooms. She had been worried that Greg would still have been annoyed with her, but to her relief it seemed as if he had totally forgotten her earlier faux pas. Oh, well, she decided, tomorrow was another day and she had no doubt that it was going to be as challenging as today had been. As long as she didn't say the wrong thing again in front of Greg, Kirsty ruminated, although a tiny voice wondered why the thought of upsetting Greg should bother her so much.

The Jeep rattled its way over the dusty and bumpy dirt roads. They had left the tarred road almost an hour before and this road showed no sign of ever coming to an end. Kirsty almost felt travel-sick from being bounced around like a sack of potatoes. But there was no way she was going to complain.

Greg had knocked on her door at five-thirty that morning, just as she had emerged from the shower.

Wordlessly he had held out a flask of coffee and bowl of fruit salad.

As she had stood at the door, her hair wrapped in a towel turban and her thin dressing-gown clinging to her still damp body, she'd noticed Greg's appreciative look as he'd taken in her curves.

Seconds later she'd thought she must have imagined it. Greg's eyebrows had drawn together as he'd frowned at her.

'I thought at the very least you'd be dressed by now,' he said shortly. 'When you didn't appear for breakfast I thought I'd better check you were up.'

'I am not in the habit of sleeping in. For heaven's sake, Dr du Toit, I thought we'd agreed that you were going to stop treating me as if I were a child. And,' she added quickly, seeing him open his mouth to interrupt, 'I'm afraid that checking that I'm up and ready for work counts. As does making sure I'm fed.'

He had the grace to look slightly sheepish. He gave a lopsided smile and Kirsty was dismayed to feel her heart somersault.

'I know we agreed, but then I realised I hadn't told you the village was a good couple of hours' drive away, and it might be a few hours after that before we get something to eat.'

Kirsty smiled to let him know he was forgiven. It had been longer than she cared to admit, even to herself, since anyone had considered her needs.

'I'll just throw some clothes on if you want to

come in. I haven't sorted my hairdryer so I'll just plait my hair. All in all it'll take me five minutes.' She was about to turn and head for her bedroom when she remembered the coffee. She took it from his unresisting grip.

'The kettle's just boiled for my coffee. We can keep this for the journey.'

Now all she longed for was a cold drink of water. Her mouth felt as if a herd of elephants had set up home. The dust from the dirt road had penetrated everywhere.

She and Greg were alone in the Jeep. The nurse who was to accompany them had left earlier with Thandi and Johan, who had been responsible for drilling the wells. Greg had explained that they all stayed a few miles away from the hospital compound and it was easier for them to travel together.

'I don't know why I bothered showering,' Kirsty muttered, 'and as for washing my hair, well…'

Greg's glance at her was fleeting.

'You'll get used to it.'

'I'm sure I will.' She looked around at the sunburnt ochre hills that gave the dust its reddish hue. 'It is beautiful. Stark, but beautiful. You can imagine it being like this since the beginning of time. Oh, look!' In her excitement she tugged at Greg's arm. 'Over there!'

In the distance a herd of buck, as graceful as ballerinas, danced across the veld. Every so often they would soar into the sky as if for the sheer joy of it.

Greg grinned. 'Impala.' He looked at her intently, as if struck by something.

'I think I must have been here too long. I've become so accustomed to the beauty of Africa I have stopped seeing it. You'll have to visit one of the game reserves when you have time off,' he said.

'Do I get time off?' Kirsty said, feigning disbelief. And just as Greg's brows drew together she winked at him. Suddenly he laughed, sounding surprised.

'Touché,' he said.

A short time later the Jeep drew into the village. A group of children came running towards them, yodelling and laughing. Women with baskets of firewood balanced precariously on their heads walked between small huts made of mud. Kirsty couldn't imagine how the women managed to balance the heavy loads on their heads as if they weighed nothing. They could teach the catwalk models of New York a thing or two, she thought.

Over to one side Kirsty saw a makeshift tent where a number of women and children squatted patiently. Kirsty could make out the tall figure of Sister Matabele as she weighed babies and small children. While she took in the scene around her, she helped Greg to unload the Jeep.

'This is one of the more fortunate villages,' Greg informed Kirsty as they carried supplies of vaccinations and medical equipment over to the tent. 'Operation Health finished putting in a well here a couple of weeks ago. For the first time ever the villagers have access to fresh water all year round. Not just for drinking and cooking, but for bathing and washing clothes. At this time of year the streams have all but dried up and the water is sluggish and contaminated, and in the past, for lack of any other options, they were forced to bathe and wash clothes in what little water there was, then use the same water to drink. Now, however, they have enough clean water for all their needs, including irrigation. Now they can grow crops.' He pointed to a group of women bent low in the distance. 'See there? That will be their first real crop of mealies and vegetables. Starvation and gastroenteritis will soon be a thing of the past.' Kirsty could see how pleased he was. 'Clean water and education, that's what really makes the difference.'

'Where are all the men?' Kirsty asked. Apart from one or two elderly men sitting by the doors of the huts, it was mainly women and children in the village.

'They leave for the cities. It's where the work is, and the money. Some send money back, but often that eventually dries up and the women are left to do what they can.' As they had been talking they had been setting out their supplies on a table. Greg snapped on a pair of gloves.

'OK, Kirsty, we'll start at the beginning of the queue. Nurse Matabele has already triaged the patients. When I first arrived at the hospital a child died while the mother was waiting her turn.'

'How awful,' Kirsty said, aghast. 'How on

earth could that have happened? Why didn't she insist on being seen earlier?'

'The child had already been ill for a week. Then the mother walked with the child for four days to get to the hospital. I guess she thought everything would be all right if she just waited her turn. The women aren't used to making a fuss. So now we make sure all the patients are triaged when we do these outlying clinics. Maybe this way we can save one or two who might otherwise have died.'

For a moment Greg looked into the distance. Maybe he wasn't so good at keeping his emotions tightly under control after all. But there was no more time for talk. Kirsty and Greg divided the patients between them. Soon it became obvious that the easier patients had been allocated to Kirsty: the children and elderly who needed vaccinations or vitamins. But quickly Kirsty became immersed in the steady stream of patients, who, just like those they saw in the hospital clinic, waited patiently, grateful for the smallest effort. Kirsty found it very humbling. More than once, confronted with the desperate poverty and deprivation, she had cringed, recalling her lifestyle back in the UK. She had taken so much for granted. How often had she spent more on a pair of shoes than most here had to spend on food for months?

During an examination of an elderly woman Kirsty became aware of a nurse by her side.

'Dr Greg asks if you can go over to him,' the nurse said. 'I'll see to these patients in the meantime.'

Kirsty found Greg examining a boy of about three or four.

She drew in a sharp intake of breath when she saw the young boy's arms. They were covered in burns, at least second-degree, Kirsty thought, and the right arm had swollen grotesquely from just above the elbow to the fingertips. Greg was asking the boy, who stood with wet eyes, to try and flex his fingers. The child was finding it impossible.

'Dr Boucher,' Greg greeted her, barely glancing up. 'I would be interested to hear what you think of the case.' He said something to the nurse aide who scurried off.

'This little chap—Mathew is his English

name—pulled a paraffin heater over onto himself a couple of days ago.' He went on, 'His mother took him to the local healer who prescribed some herbs which haven't improved matters. What do you think?' While he was talking he pulled a packet of sweets from his pocket and proffered them to his patient, who took them with a shy smile of thanks.

Kirsty felt her stomach clench as she examined the boy. There were some burns to the chest, but they were mainly superficial. He had also been splashed with the burning paraffin on the lower part of his face. It was his arms that had been most badly affected. To make matters worse, the burns had blistered and were badly infected. Kirsty knew that the burns on their own were significant, but add infection to the equation and the boy's chances of a full recovery were severely diminished.

'Second-, possibly third-degree burns to the arms and face. First-degree burns to the chest. The arms are infected and clearly Mathew has restricted movement in his right hand.' Kirsty made notes as she called out her assessment.

Kirsty looked at Greg when she had finished

and was surprised to see his jaw clenching, his mouth set in a grim line. As he looked down at his own hand, flexing it and failing to achieve full inflection, Kirsty knew he was reminded of his own injuries.

'Why didn't she bring him to us at the hospital when it first happened?' Kirsty asked. 'He needs to be started on IV antibiotics and hospitalised straight away to get that infection cleared up. As for his hand…' she shook her head, averting her eyes from the mother '…it's possible that he may have lost full use permanently.'

'And how was his mother going to get him to hospital? It's thirty miles away at a guess and she would have had to carry him every step of the way. At least the healer lives in her village. She knew we were coming today and decided to wait. We can't blame her for doing what she thought was best. However, you're right—he does need to be in hospital, but first we have to sort out that hand.'

The nurse aide returned, carrying a procedure pack which she opened while Greg spoke in quiet, urgent tones to the mother. It was only when Greg picked up a scalpel that Kirsty realised with horrified fascination what he was about to do.

'You can't operate here,' she said.

'I can and I will. If you don't want to watch, go back to your patients, otherwise hold the boy's arm firmly for me.'

'But without anaesthetic, without analgesia? He's only little, Greg,' Kirsty pleaded.

Greg looked at her steadily. 'You need to trust me on this, Kirsty. But if you want, you can leave now. If you stay, I need to know I can rely on you. Can I?'

For a moment Kirsty held his eyes. Did she trust him? As a doctor, unquestionably. It was only his apparent lack of compassion that bothered her. Was he immune to the suffering and pain he was about to inflict on this child who gazed up at him with unwavering trust? Had his own experiences blunted him to the point where the outcome was all that mattered?

As if he could read Kirsty's mind, Greg said gently, 'It won't hurt him, I promise you. The burns are so deep the nerves have been damaged. If I thought that it would hurt him, or if there was any other way, believe me, I would take it. But if there is any chance at all of saving function in the hand, I have to do this here and now.'

Kirsty nodded, knowing it mattered little to Greg what she thought.

Smoothly, without the slightest hesitation, Greg drew the scalpel across the charred skin along the length of the boy's forearm. Immediately the flesh parted, revealing the pink muscle underneath, and the hand began to lose its dusky hue.

Mathew flinched, but more out of surprise, Kirsty realised, than pain.

Greg straightened. 'That will do for the time being. When we get him to hospital, we can tidy things up.'

Once more Kirsty could detect bleakness in his eyes. She wondered if she'd misread him. Could it be that he wasn't as detached from his patients as he'd have her believe? Or was it just this little boy with his horrible burns in particular? Did he remind him of his own child?

'I'll go back with him if you like,' Kirsty volunteered, as she sought a vein in an undamaged limb for a drip. The nurse began bandaging the boy's burns. Once she had finished dressing his burns and they had started him on IV antibiotics, it would just be a matter of keeping him comfortable and pain-free until they got him to the hospital.

'No,' Greg said abruptly, without looking up from his notes. 'Sister Matabele will go with him. She has more experience.' He looked up just in time to notice Kirsty wince. 'It's for the best, Kirsty,' he said not unkindly. 'You need to be here so you can learn. With me to keep an eye on you. The child needs to be in the safest pair of hands. It means that you'll have to do what Sister Matabele would have done, as well as helping me.'

How patronising, Kirsty fumed, but knew better than to argue. It wasn't as if Greg was asking her. It was clear that as far as the job went he was in charge and would brook no arguments. Everyone would do as he said or heaven help them.

Kirsty worked tirelessly throughout the rest of the afternoon. Despite the new well, there were still children and adults suffering the long-term effects of malnutrition. There were also sores which had turned septic and a large number of patients requiring antibiotics.

Greg worked alongside her, checking her diagnoses without implying that he had any reservations about her medical skills. Often he would catch her eye and nod encouragement. Kirsty could feel her confidence growing under his supervision. Although there were some occasions when she had to ask for his help, he was always patient. Whatever else she thought of him, Kirsty realised she had found a fine teacher in Dr du Toit.

It was mid-afternoon by the time the last patient had been seen and Kirsty's stomach was beginning to growl with hunger.

'Food?' she suggested to Greg and laughed at his look of surprise. 'Whatever you might think,' she said, 'I do like to eat.'

'Is it that time already?' Greg asked. He sniffed the air appreciatively. 'Mmm, I think lunch is ready.'

They had no sooner finished clearing up when one of the women called them over to a circle of logs, arranged as seats, around a fire. In the centre a buxom woman with a wide smile stirred a large black pot suspended over the burning coals. Kirsty and Greg and the rest of the team were urged to sit by the woman and were handed battered tin plates.

Greg and Kirsty shared one of the logs. Given Greg's large frame, it was a tight fit and she was uncomfortably conscious of his muscular thigh against hers. For some reason her heart was beating faster than usual. Just the heat and hunger she reassured herself.

'Are we going to eat their food?' Kirsty whispered, perturbed.

'Why?' Greg asked. 'Not to your cosmopolitan taste?' The frown was back. 'You'll eat it whether you like it or not.'

'Good God, Dr du Toit,' Kirsty said exasperated, 'of course it's not the food. I love trying new tastes. It's just…' his eyes followed hers as she looked around the village '…they don't seem to have enough for themselves, let alone us. Couldn't we have brought something with us?'

She smiled her thanks as one of the women

ladled a thick stew and some white stuff that looked like a mix between porridge and rice onto her tin plate.

Greg turned to face her and his face relaxed into a smile. Once again Kirsty was aware of her pulse going out of kilter.

'We did bring food. And it was gratefully received. But it's important to the villagers that they share what little they have with us. They are a proud people and it's the only way they can thanks us. You have to trust me on this.'

'I have to trust you on a load of things,' Kirsty said. But she too smiled to show there were no hard feelings. 'But what exactly is it I'm about to eat?' she whispered

'Oxtail stew and mealie pap, a type of porridge made from maize meal,' Greg answered. 'Mealies are the staple food in this part of Africa, eaten at every meal. It grows fairly easily, given a water supply. And it's nutritious and cheap. Try some with a bit of the stew.'

Kirsty did as he'd suggested and was pleasantly surprised. The porridge didn't taste of very much on its own, but with the stew it was tasty enough. Besides, she was ravenous. She would have eaten almost anything.

Greg ate with the same concentration and efficiency he seemed to do everything. She decided that now was not the time for small talk and instead let her gaze travel around the village. Most of the work had stopped for lunch and the villagers sat around in groups, chatting and casting openly curious looks in Kirsty's direction. A group of children ran through the village, squealing happily as they used sticks to propel old tyres and race each other. Kirsty wondered absent-mindedly where the tyres had come from. Apart from the clinic's and the Operation Health's cars, there were no other vehicles in sight.

She handed her empty plate back to one of the women, indicating with sign language that, no, she wouldn't take any more, she was full up, it was quite delicious and thank you so much. Greg was deep in conversation with Johan and Thandi from Operation Health so Kirsty thought she might take the opportunity to explore.

Just as she stood, she was startled by a high-pitched cry as one of the women who had been peeling vegetables dropped her knife and clutched her hand.

Before anyone else could react, Kirsty was at the stricken woman's side. The woman was on her feet, moaning with pain. 'Let me see,' Kirsty said, putting out her hand. 'Please,' she said as the woman hesitated.

'Stop right there.' Greg's voice halted her in her tracks. Her hand froze mid-air. She turned to see him striding towards her while pulling on latex gloves. 'Don't touch her, Dr Boucher,' he said as he reached them. Kirsty let her hands drop to her sides. What had she been thinking? She watched as Greg quickly examined the woman's hand. 'It will need suturing,' he said to Kirsty. 'Which you can do, once you have double-gloved.'

'Of course,' she said, feeling the colour rush to her cheeks. 'I'm sorry. It was an instinctive reaction.'

'You never ever touch anyone, particularly someone who is bleeding, unless you are double-gloved,' Greg ground out between clenched teeth. 'The risk of infection is too great. Surely you were taught that?'

'Yes, of course, but…' Although Kirsty knew there was little she could say in her defence, at least he should understand it had been a normal reaction to another human being in distress.

'No buts. It's not only your own life you put at risk but your patients'. Remember that. Now, let's get this hand sutured.' Before she could reply he had walked off.

Kirsty felt her eyes smart, followed quickly by a wave of anger. That kind of attitude had gone out with the ark, surely. But she knew she had almost made a mistake and was deeply embarrassed. Just when she thought she was making a good impression—a medical impression that was, of course. She didn't care what other sort of impression she had been making—or did she? Why else would she feel as if she had taken a blow to the solar plexus? Did it really matter what Greg thought of her—apart from her medical skills? Unfortunately a little voice was saying that it did. It was beginning to matter a whole lot more than Kirsty would have thought possible.

* * *

Later, the vehicles were packed and ready for the return journey. The sun was beginning to drop in the sky and if they wanted to make it back to the hospital compound before dark, Greg knew they should get going. He looked around for Kirsty, realising the last he had seen of her had been when she had gone off to suture the woman with the knife wound, but that had been a long time ago. He felt a little guilty about earlier. He had been a bit brusque after what had been a genuine attempt to help. But, damn it, he wanted her to do well. There was something about that look in those green eyes, a look of defiance mixed with vulnerability, that seemed to be getting under his skin. Why she seemed to have this effect on him, he had no idea. He had worked with countless doctors before and had never been drawn to any of them the way he was drawn to Kirsty. It had been one of his unwritten rules—never get involved with his junior colleagues. He wasn't above having affairs, but never with his medical subordinates.

Suddenly the full realisation of what he'd been thinking hit him. He had been thinking of Kirsty as a woman he'd like to have in his bed. She was someone who was beginning to make him think that some rules could be broken. He almost groaned aloud. Kirsty Boucher was becoming a complication he could do without. Maybe he should try and convince her to go home. After all, he'd be doing her a favour. She obviously wasn't cut out for the harsh reality of Africa. She'd be much better off back in the UK in a city hospital, close to friends and family. And he, if not the hospital, would be better off without her, too. But for now he needed to find her and take her home.

CHAPTER FIVE

GREG eventually found Kirsty where he least expected to find her, in the fields, working alongside the women who were back at work, planting the next season's crops. The stillness was punctuated by the sound of the women singing, their beautiful ululating voices carrying through the air. Every now and again one of them would break off and bend towards Kirsty with a laugh and correct her movements. Kirsty had rolled up her khaki chinos to protect the bottoms from the damp soil. But her once crisply white blouse was now more of a pinkish brown and she had undone a couple of extra buttons against the heat.

Greg was dismayed to find himself stir as she bent, copying the women's actions and offering him a tantalising glimpse of her breasts. He called out to get her attention. She looked up at the sound of his voice, pushing a strand of auburn hair away with the heel of her hand. The gesture left a grubby smear across her cheek. Greg had to fight hard to resist the temptation to rub the mark away with a finger. Her face was glistening with her efforts, her cheeks flushed, and she was ruefully examining a broken nail, but Greg thought she looked more beautiful than ever.

'I hope you don't mind, but I thought, since we had finished work and you still had unfinished business, I would lend a hand here.' She indicated her companions with a sweep of her hand. 'They have all been so patient with me and have been trying to teach me the odd word here and there.'

'It's time to go if we want to get back before dark.'

'I'd like to stay a little longer. We're almost finished. We've only got a couple more rows.' She looked so determined Greg didn't have the heart to refuse her, even if it meant they were late leaving.

'OK, then,' he said, pulling off his shirt to expose tanned skin and well-developed muscles. 'I'll help. That way, we'll be finished quicker.' Ignoring the giggles of the women, he took a hoe from one of them and set about furrowing rows with a will.

Thirty back-breaking minutes later they had finished. Kirsty looked down at her hands in horror. It would take a week of Shona's sought-after manicures to get her blistered hands back into shape. And what had been one lamented broken nail had turned into four. She looked up from her doleful scrutiny of her hands to find Greg's eyes on her, his expression inscrutable except for—surely it couldn't be—a flash of approval in his eyes.

'Let's get going,' he said gruffly. 'We've wasted enough time as it is.'

'I need a moment to wash,' Kirsty said. 'I couldn't bear the journey home caked in this dust. And I'm pretty sweaty, too. I don't think I'll make a very pleasant passenger.'

The expression in Greg's eyes changed. This time Kirsty could have sworn she saw a glint of amusement.

'Fancy a quick shower before we leave?'

This was a sudden change of heart, coming from Greg. Kirsty frowned, dismissing her suspicions. She did need to wash and cool down.

'OK, then. Come with me. I'll show you how we shower African style.'

He led her over to one of the few trees that provided shelter to the villagers from the worst of the sun. Kirsty could see that some sort of rope and bucket contraption had been rigged in one of the trees but, nonplussed, she looked around for even the suggestion of a shower.

'Wait here.' Greg led her by the arm to a spot beneath the tree.

Kirsty did as she was told, glad even for the limited relief from the heat the shade of the tree offered.

Then, without warning, she was soaked in icy cold water that was falling from above her. Spluttering and gasping, she could see Greg grinning broadly. Suddenly she was furious. She stormed up to Greg, grabbing an abandoned blanket from a rock as she passed.

'Highly amusing, I'm sure,' she said through gritted teeth. 'I wanted a shower but not fully dressed or in full view of everyone. Have you not had enough fun at my expense?'

'I'm sorry. I shouldn't have sprung it on you,

but it is how we all shower in the bush. Usually with fewer clothes on, it has to be said.'

'Not funny.' Kirsty glared, aware that she was the object of much amusement as all the villagers looked her way. A group of children pointed, covering giggles behind small hands. As quickly as it had come, the anger left her. She did feel wonderfully cool. And her clothes were already beginning to dry. 'I'll get you back one day,' she admonished, smiling to show she bore no malice. 'I am a patient woman with a long memory.'

The sun was setting as they left the village, bathing the roads and hills in a wash of red. The villagers turned out to wave them off, singing and dancing. As she waved back, Kirsty felt a lump in her throat. Africa wasn't turning out the way she had expected. Although in her haste to leave Glasgow she hadn't, if she were honest, given much thought at all to what she had been coming to. It had been a bit of a shock when she had arrived, but she hadn't been prepared for the country and its people getting under her skin.

She turned to the man sitting beside her. In the

gathering darkness his scars were almost invisible. Indeed, Kirsty thought she could no longer imagine him without them. To her they had become an essential part of the man. Part of who he was.

But did they remind him of his wife and child every time he looked in the mirror? How could they not?

The dusk gave Kirsty the courage to ask, 'What was she like—your wife?'

For a moment she thought he was going to tell her to mind her own business again, but instead he looked thoughtful. He started to speak, slowly at first, as if the words were painful.

'We met at university. She was studying English and drama and I was a medical student. We both belonged to the fencing club, but she was much better than I could ever be.' He smiled, remembering. 'She was beautiful, but more than that she had an aura about her that drew people to her. She wanted to be an actress, and had already been offered a part in a play in her last year of university, but she fell pregnant and that was that. There was no other way for her except to have our child and support us while I finished my medical degree. She said she could always return to acting when I started earning. But—that wasn't to be. The opportunities never came around again.' He closed his eyes for a brief moment as if to shut away the memories.

He continued, his voice husky with regret. 'I owed her so much. She never complained, never resented the hand life dealt her, even when she was so often alone with our child in those early years while I was completing my training. The hours were horrendous back then. You guys have no idea how much easier you have it today.'

'I know,' Kirsty said. 'But the shorter hours have their own disadvantages. It is much more difficult to get the experience. Most of us feel we're qualified almost before time. We've done about a third of the time our predecessors did, and we don't always feel ready.'

'Is that what brought you out here? I know someone pulled a few strings. I have to be honest, I didn't believe you had the experience for this job. I was against employing you for that reason.

And...' he looked sideways at her '...despite your performance so far, I still think I was right.'

Kirsty looked down at her hands. She was gripping them tightly together. She hadn't fully appreciated until now how much she wanted to stay. And not just because of Robbie.

'You have every right to think that,' she said slowly. 'I don't really have enough experience for this job but, as you said last night, none of our training in Western city hospitals can really prepare any of us for working in Third World rural communities. Believe me, I didn't come here to practise my medical skills, although I am desperate to learn as much as I can, but only so I can be of some use. No, I came here because...' As soon as the last words were out of her mouth Kirsty would have done anything to take them back. If Greg knew the true reason she had come, his worst fears about her would be confirmed.

'One of the reasons I came here was because of my father. You've probably heard of him? Professor Keith Boucher?'

Greg shook his head slightly. 'Doesn't ring a bell.'

'Well, you must be one of the few people in

the Western medical world who doesn't know who he is.'

'Wait a minute,' Greg said as the penny dropped. 'Professor Keith Boucher.' Of course he knew who he was. He had simply never connected the charismatic world reknowned professor with the under-confident Kirsty.

'No. I'm afraid I never made the connection. It didn't cross my mind.'

'I can see why it wouldn't,' Kirsty said with a slight twist of her mouth. 'We are nothing like each other.' She paused. 'I hardly saw my father as I was growing up. He was always speaking at one international conference or another or building up his private practice. I wasn't always an only child. My mother and younger sister were killed in a car accident when I was ten. From then on I saw even less of him. It was as if he couldn't bear to be in the same room as me. Sometimes I wondered if he wished it had been me who had died instead of them.' Her voice trembled slightly before she managed to get it under control.

Greg reached across and squeezed Kirsty's hand.

'I'm so sorry, Kirsty.'

'I always felt guilty,' she went on, 'for not dying. Can you believe that?' She glanced across at Greg, who nodded almost imperceptibly. The memories were flooding back. The anguish of losing her mother and sister—then the rejection by her father. The feelings of being alone and unwanted.

'It was as if he no longer had a reason to come home. So I tried to make him proud of me. I guess I wanted to make him notice me, so I worked hard, got top grades…'

'And became a doctor,' Greg finished for her. 'Not the best of reasons perhaps?'

'I became a doctor *despite* my father, not *because* of my father. Don't you see the last thing I wanted to do was end up in the same field as him? One in which I could only ever be compared unfavourably. Where people would always have unrealistic expectations of me. But in the end medicine was what I wanted to do. I needed to become a doctor. There was no other career that felt right.'

And, Kirsty thought bitterly, it was probably

the reason Robbie had wanted to marry her. The reflected glory of being Professor Boucher's son-in-law. If he had really loved her he would have shared her longing to have children. After her lonely childhood, she knew, when the time was right, that she wanted to have at least a couple of kids. Why bother with marriage otherwise? But Robbie, it seemed, had had entirely different plans.

'And your mother? What was she like?' Greg prompted.

'She was also a doctor—I come from a family of high achievers. I didn't see all that much of her either before she died. But at least I knew she loved me,' she said.

Greg looked at her expectantly, waiting for her to go on. But Kirsty decided she had revealed as much of her private life as she was prepared to. Too much, in fact.

'So what about your parents?' she asked, determined to steer the conversation away from herself. She was also genuinely curious about her companion.

'Both alive and well. They live in Cape Town.

I don't see them as often as I'd like, but we keep in touch.'

Kirsty fell silent as they drew up outside their living quarters. She could hardly believe the journey was over. The last couple of hours had flown. Suddenly now they were back she felt shy again, mortified at how easily he had steered the conversation back round to her and embarrassed that she had revealed so much of herself. Had it been because she really needed his good opinion? In the same way she still sought her father's? Or was it because she needed to let him know that she knew what it was like to lose the people you loved most in the world?

Greg leant over to open the door for her and she could feel the heat from his body. For a moment she had the ridiculous notion she could turn towards him and rest in his arms. She'd feel protected there. But in the next instant her head cleared. She didn't need protection. She was more than able to look after herself, despite what everyone seemed to think. And being here, coping—and she *was* coping—was proving it. And as for her and Greg, the idea was laughable.

The man was still in love with his wife. That much a blind man, or woman, could see.

'Home,' Greg said. 'I'll see you at dinner?'

Kirsty shook her head. 'I don't think so. I'm still pretty full after that late lunch and, besides, Sarah was going to town and said she'd pick up some supplies for me. I'm sure I'll find something to snack on if I get hungry later,' she said pointedly, before Greg could open his mouth. She was tired, not particularly hungry and for some reason she felt the need to have some time on her own to get her thoughts in order. Talking about her father and thinking about her mother and sister had dredged up feelings that had left her emotionally drained.

'Suit yourself,' Greg said. 'I'll see you tomorrow.' He lingered for a moment, as if about to say something else, but then with a final puzzled look he disappeared into his own house.

Sarah had indeed been shopping and she or someone else had thoughtfully stocked Kirsty's fridge and cupboards with bread, butter, eggs and cheese, as well as fruit, fresh salad, vegetables and pasta. Everything she needed. The house felt cool now that the sun had set and Kirsty shivered a little. She showered and changed into her pyjamas. She thought she'd go to bed with her book. It had been an early start and she knew she could expect a busy day the following day.

No sooner had she found the scene in the detective novel she had started on the flight when the phone rang with an unremitting jangle. Kirsty couldn't ever remember seeing a phone that looked quite as antiquated outside a museum. It was made of black Bakelite and instead of buttons had a handle on the side. If you wanted to make a telephone call you had to rotate the arm several times until someone at the hospital switchboard picked up. You would then be connected. Kirsty hadn't as yet attempted to make a call—after all, who would she ring? She had heard the others complain bitterly about aborted calls and most used their mobiles. She, on the other hand, still needed to get hers modified.

As she picked up the phone she wondered who could be ringing. Perhaps it was Sarah, checking she had got her supplies. With a flicker of dismay

Kirsty remembered she had intended to pop over to Sarah's house to thank her. She had simply forgotten in her tiredness.

But it wasn't Sarah's voice she heard. It was Robbie's. Her heart leapt, then fell as she recognised his voice. She wasn't ready to speak to him.

'How did you find me?' she said. 'I made my friends promise not to tell you. Whoever did so had no right.'

'It wasn't any of them Kirsty. It was your father.'

'Dad.' She should have known. He had been unsympathetic when Kirsty had told him that there wasn't to be a wedding. Although she hadn't told him the reason, if he knew anything about her, he'd have known that she wouldn't have broken off her engagement lightly. A father who cared would have supported her decision unquestionably. But he hadn't said much, just made it obvious he disapproved. Yet for the first time she could remember he was getting involved in her life. Once that would have made her happy. Now it made her angry.

'He had no right to tell you either. It's none of his business. If I wanted to speak to you, I would have called.'

'Look here, Kirsty. We need to talk. You never gave me the chance to explain. You just refused to let me near you and then ran off. Come home. We can talk about it. Sort it out. Please, darling, I need you.'

'Need my father more likely,' Kirsty ground out. 'Do you think I haven't realised that he's the reason why you wanted to marry me? Getting a share in his private practice must have seemed like an excellent reason to get married,' she said bitterly.

'My wanting to marry you has nothing to do with your father,' Robbie protested. 'I love you. And you love me. Come home,' he said again, 'so we can sort this all out.'

'You've a funny way of showing someone you love them,' Kirsty said. 'And as for my loving you—well, maybe I thought I was in love with you, but I was mistaken. Maybe I thought I wanted the life you were offering to me, but I'm not so sure now. I just know there is no going back for us. I'm sorry, Robbie. Really I am. But you can't say you didn't bring all this on yourself. I'm pretty certain Dad will honour his promise to involve you in his private practice.

He's not the kind of man to allow a small matter like loyalty get in the way of a good business arrangement. So I wouldn't worry on that score.'

The line started to crackle with static electricity, drowning out Robbie's protests. She could just make out the words 'mistake' and 'need to see you' before the line went dead. Kirsty was relieved. There wasn't any point in continuing the conversation. When she had found Robbie in bed with another woman she had thought her heart would break. Until that moment she had believed that she had found someone who loved her unconditionally. How wrong she had been. Robbie's betrayal had made her feel fury, hurt and humiliation in equal degrees. Running away had seemed the only answer. She couldn't have endured seeing him every day at the hospital, knowing that she was the cause of the whispers and sly glances. So she had run away. And it dawned on her she had barely thought about Robbie since she'd arrived! Admittedly there had been too much going on, but perhaps she hadn't been as in love with him as she had thought?

Maybe he had done them both a favour. It was

a novel idea, but one that made sense. Perhaps Robbie's actions had prevented her from making the worst mistake of her life.

Kirsty could have only been asleep for a couple of hours when something ran across her face. She jumped out of bed, swatting at her arms and legs in a frenzy lest the wretched beast—whatever it was—was still attached to her. Cursing out loud—she *hated* creepy-crawlies—she did a one-legged dance across the room until she reached the light switch. Even in the full glare of the bare light bulb there was no evidence of her visitor. Heart still pounding, Kirsty made a thorough search of the room, through her bed-clothes, under the bed and in the cupboards, but whatever it was had gone. Or so she thought until she looked upwards.

There, on the ceiling, a few feet above her pillow, almost looking at her, was the most enormous and certainly the hairiest spider she had ever seen. She felt ill at the thought that this was what had woken her up. There was no way she could stay in this house with the spider. Had she really thought barely hours ago that she could fall in love with this country? She must have been under the influence of some hallucinatory drug. She just didn't do countries that sheltered spiders that big.

Looking at her watch, she confirmed the time. It was almost midnight. What was she to do?

Seeking a weapon, her eyes alighted on the floor brush. It wasn't much, but perhaps she could use it to chase the spider out of her house. She didn't particularly care where it went as long as it wasn't within two hundred feet of her. Carefully manipulating the brush, she nudged the spider with the handle. At first it refused to budge and then without warning it dropped to the floor before scuttling over her foot. Kirsty screamed, thrashing frantically at her feet. Before she could recover, Greg appeared in her room, bare-chested, tugging at the zip of his jeans.

'What the hell's going on?'

'A spider—huge.' She gestured, with the broom clenched defensively in front of her. 'I think it's hiding under the bed.'

Her eyes slid briefly to Greg as he let out an incredulous snort of laughter.

'A *spider?* God, Kirsty, I thought you were being murdered.'

'It's enormous,' she said, backing out of the bedroom, still holding the broom. 'I've never seen anything like it.'

Greg's lips twitched. 'All that noise because of a spider?'

'Believe me,' Kirsty said indignantly, 'this was no ordinary spider. It's clearly mutated or something. It's at least the size of a rat.' She shivered with revulsion.

His eyes crinkled and the small smile broadened into a grin. Flustered, she dropped her eyes and then became riveted by the sight of his naked torso, muscles taut, the skin golden except for the path of dark hair disappearing below the waistband of his jeans.

'Trust me, big spiders are usually perfectly harmless. It's the small ones you have to watch out for. These are the ones that can be, well, venomous.'

'I don't believe you. And, anyway, I don't care.

Either that spider goes or I do. There is no way I'm spending the night with that monster if there's any likelihood it's still under this roof.'

There was no disguising Greg's amusement now. 'You'll have to get used to it, Kirsty. Africa is chock-full of insects. Many of them perfectly harmless.' But when she failed to budge he relented. 'OK, let's see if we can evict your guest so we can all get some sleep.'

Despite an extensive hunt, Kirsty's eight-legged visitor remained elusive. While they searched Kirsty burned with mortification. More evidence, she thought grimly, that she was unsuited to working in Africa. As if he'd needed any more. But it wasn't fair. She couldn't help her phobia. She searched frantically for a solution. No matter how silly and pathetic he thought her, there was absolutely no chance she was spending the night in her house. Perhaps she could intrude on Sarah and Jamie? As a woman, Sarah was bound to sympathise.

'I'm sorry,' Greg said at last. 'We aren't getting anywhere with this. You probably frightened it half to death and it made its escape while the going was good. I'm sure it's more scared of you than you are of it.'

'I don't care what you say. I am not spending the night here.' Kirsty folded her arms across her chest and anyone who knew her well could have told from the mutinous set of her mouth that there was no way she was going to change her mind.

Greg stepped closer, his eyes narrowing. 'Are you suggesting that you sleep at my place?' he asked, a dangerous glint in his eyes.

Kirsty fought the temptation to take a step back. She refused to let this man ridicule or intimidate her. He must already think that she was some pathetic female who liked nothing better than to lean on a strong man's shoulder. Unfortunately, she shuddered, it was easy to see how he might have gained that impression.

'Don't be ridiculous,' Kirsty replied indignantly. 'I said I had a phobia about spiders, not that I was off my head. It'll take more than a spider—no matter how huge—to get me into bed with you,' she said, her temper rising. The moment the words were out she wished she could have bitten them back. The man was still her boss after all, although thinking of him as anything other than a sexual predator was proving difficult.

Greg raised an eyebrow. 'Who said anything about getting into bed with me? I meant stay at *my place,* that was all. Although now that you suggest it, maybe that's not such a bad idea.' His eyes raked over her body.

Once again Kirsty felt the hot tide of embarrassment suffuse her body. She had forgotten that she was wearing very little, and self-consciously brought her arms up to cover her body. Quickly she scooped her lightweight dressing-gown from the bottom of the bed.

Idiot, idiot, idiot, she berated herself mentally. Was there any way at all she could give Greg a worse impression of her?

'I was suggesting no such thing,' she said hotly, shrugging into the gown, after giving it a thorough shake. Luckily, before she could say anything more she noticed the wide grin on Greg's face. It was amazing how humour transformed his face. She hadn't thought of him as having a sense of humour. Up until now he had seemed, well, a little taciturn.

'OK, OK. You've had your fun at my expense—yet again,' she said, attempting a grin of her own. Maybe she could convince him she had been kidding, too?

However, *nothing* was going to make her sleep in this room. She would keep vigil in one of the chairs in the sitting room. Naturally there wasn't anything as civilised as a sofa in her accommodation. She could always curl her feet underneath her. In the morning she'd get someone, anyone, to give the house a clean sweep from top to bottom.

Greg must have seen her uncertainty. He assumed the slightly exasperated expression that she seemed to inspire.

'You have my bed,' he said. 'Alone,' he added pointedly, as Kirsty started to object. 'I'll sleep here. In yours. At least, that way we'll both get some rest some time tonight. I don't think there are any monster spiders in my house—but I'm afraid that's a chance you'll have to take. Unless, of course, you'd rather I kept you company, although I can't guarantee you'd actually be protected from danger.' Once more the amused look was back, but this time there was something else, something that Kirsty couldn't quite read.

'That's very kind of you,' she said stiffly. 'If you're sure you don't mind having my bed for the night?' She lifted her chin. 'I am well aware that you find this perfectly ridiculous and completely incomprehensible. I can only assure you, that it won't happen again. Now, if I can just collect my toothbrush, and I'm sure there are one or two things you'll need from your place, I'll say goodnight and let you get some sleep.'

'I don't need anything. I was in bed when I heard you scream,' Greg replied. 'I'm pretty bushed. All I want right now is a bed and a few hours' sleep.'

'Goodnight, then, Dr du Toit,' Kirsty said politely as she left the room, knowing all the while it was far too late to try to remind them both of their professional relationship.

Hours later Greg was still wide awake. He had thought he'd fall sleep the minute his head hit the pillow, but he hadn't allowed for the fact that the faint scent of Kirsty's perfume and the memory of her half-naked body was doing things to his libido that he truly resented. It had been a while since he had taken a woman to his bed—he was no saint, but on principle he never had affairs with colleagues—and there was something about Kirsty, a vulnerability that made her un-touchable as far as he was concerned. The women he had slept with had all known the score, that he would never marry or have children again. He would never risk the pain of loss again. Anyway, no one could replace Kathleen. He would always love her.

Or did he? His thoughts turned to Kathleen, as they did so often. Lately he had been able to think of her without the gut-wrenching anguish he'd once experienced. The guilt was still there—God knew, it would stay with him the rest of his life. Not just guilt that he had been unable to save them but guilt that he hadn't spent more time with them when he'd had the oppor-tunity. Guilt that she had abandoned her dreams for him and their child. 'I have everything I want right here,' she used to say. 'There will be plenty of time later for acting. I can always play the mother-in-law if I get too old.' She would laugh, looking up at him with her soft brown eyes. And his child, his beloved Rachel—he had missed so much of her growing up. He had always thought there would be time. If only he had known how little time there was going to be.

Cursing, Greg abandoned sleep and Kirsty's bed and strode to the window. There were no streetlights here, but the light from the moon and the sprinkle of stars lit the sky.

He breathed in the cool scent of frangipani that drifted through the open window. He loved this place, and he had found some measure of peace living and working here. Although the lack of proper facilities was frustrating, he knew that his medical skills were making a difference in a way they wouldn't anywhere else. Until Kirsty had stumbled into his life he had thought he was reasonably content. Not happy—he didn't expect to be happy ever again—but content. Now he was aware that there was something missing in his life, something that niggled at him like an itch that needed to be scratched. Maybe that was it? Greg wondered. He should break his rules, bed

Kirsty, and then perhaps the irritating itch would be gone. But somewhere deep in his soul he knew it wasn't quite that simple.

CHAPTER SIX

KIRSTY left Greg's house just as the sun was beginning to rise. She had thought she wouldn't be able to sleep in the disconcertingly masculine surroundings, but she had quickly fallen into a deep, dreamless sleep. She had felt safe in Greg's bed. She smothered a laugh. She was pretty certain nothing would dare enter without an invitation!

Her curiosity had got the better of her that morning, so she had taken a few moments to explore Greg's home. There had been little to see. It was the exact reverse of hers, with no personal items to show who lived there except for a single framed photograph. She had picked it up to examine it more closely and had recognised Greg, a smile on his scar-free face. He had an arm around a woman with a little girl on her lap. The woman could only be his wife. Her long black hair framed a delicate face. She was beautiful with an impish expression, as if she held a naughty secret. The child was instantly recognisable as Greg's. The forget-me-not blue eyes could only be his. The little girl was looking up at her parents with an expression of such utter happiness and trust it made Kirsty's heart ache. How could he bear it? she wondered.

She made the bed and returned to her own house to get ready for work. She needed to shower and dress before hitting the wards. She showered quickly and, wrapping her hair in a towel, with another one tied round her body, she slipped into her bedroom, tiptoeing so as not to disturb the man who occupied her bed. Greg was still asleep, his long limbs tangled up in the sheet as if he had been fighting demons in his dreams. He clutched a pillow in one arm as if to block out the unwelcome glare of the sun.

Kirsty looked down at him for a moment. In sleep he looked less severe, almost vulnerable, despite the small crease between his eyebrows that made it seem as if he was frowning, even in his dreams. Averting her eyes from his naked limbs, she opened her wardrobe and cringed as the doors creaked. She spun around to find Greg staring at her, his blue eyes alert and unreadable.

'I'm sorry,' she said, 'I didn't mean to wake you. I'll be out of here in a minute and you can get back to sleep.' She gathered up her clothes and made to squeeze past the bed, when without warning Greg's arm shot out and grabbed her arm.

'It's still early,' he said lazily, tugging her towards him. He slid a hand further up her arm and Kirsty shivered at his touch. Powerless to resist, she allowed herself to be drawn downward until he brushed her lips with his. A spasm of lust shot through Kirsty that made her toes curl.

'Do you always have to be half-dressed around me? I'm only human, you know,' he said, his voice low.

Kirsty pulled away from his grip. Surely the man didn't think she was deliberately parading herself in front of him? He must have an even dimmer view of her than she had imagined.

'I had to get my clothes and my watch. You were in my bedroom so I had to come in. I didn't want to wake you up, otherwise I suppose I could have yelled from outside the door and then waited until you had left my room before I went for my shower.'

'Hey, remember it wasn't me who wanted to swap beds for the night,' Greg said. 'I was perfectly fine where I was until the wail of a banshee brought me running. I don't think I can be blamed for your predicament.'

'What predicament? There is no predicament. Now, would you behave like a gentleman and let me get dressed?'

'Sure,' he drawled. 'It's time I was on the wards anyway.' Greg sat up in bed and made to pull the sheets away. Kirsty backed away, realising that, as Greg obviously slept in the nude, unless she acted pretty darn quickly, she was about to be confronted with his naked body.

'I'll leave you to it,' she said, beating a hasty retreat to the bathroom.

By the time she emerged dressed, Greg had left. Kirsty sat on one of the rickety chairs in her sitting room, sipping her coffee. What just happened there? she wondered. The image of Greg's long naked limbs kept tumbling around her head, along with the memory of his hands on her arm, the touch of his lips. She felt a frisson of heat deep in her belly. For a head-spinning moment she had wanted nothing more than to abandon all caution, accept his invitation and join him in bed. Thank God she had come to her senses in time, but she still felt shaken by the power of her reaction to his touch, to the need she had seen in his eyes. She hadn't responded to a man like this since... Well, now she thought about it—never. Not even to Robbie, she realised with some amazement. *He* had never made her feel as if she wanted nothing more than to be in his bed. Oh, she had enjoyed his love-making, so much so she had imagined herself in love with him, thought she had wanted to spend the rest of her life with him. Now she realised that what she had told Robbie last night on the phone was true. She knew with absolute certainty there would never be a future for them.

She tried to conjure up the image of the man with whom she had planned to spend the rest of her life. She could bring his face into focus, but the features she'd once thought handsome now seemed insipid and weak compared to Greg's. Although Robbie had been good company, always charming and thoughtful, keen to wine and dine her at every available opportunity. Keen to lay material things at her feet. That's what she still wanted, wasn't it? A comfortable, easy life? Why, then, did she find herself comparing Robbie and Greg?

Kirsty stood up and started to tidy away the detritus of her breakfast. It must be the backlash of feeling rejected by Robbie combined with finding herself in a new situation that was making her feel this way. That was all, she told herself firmly. She simply needed to get her hormones under control. Work. That was what she needed. Plenty of honest-to-goodness hard work that left her too exhausted to think of anything else. And, she thought wryly, there was no shortage of that here.

Kirsty eased her aching back and pushed a strand of damp hair from her forehead. A swim would be lovely right now, she thought, but there were still over twenty patients in the clinic waiting to see her.

The days had settled into a routine. Work, then a couple of hours study followed by an early night. She had seen a variety of illnesses, injuries and diseases in the hospital and her confidence was continuing to grow. She had spent time with all the medical staff on the wards, with the exception of Greg, who since the spider episode seemed to be avoiding her. She didn't know whether she was sorry or relieved about that. Mainly relieved, she thought on reflection. For some reason, which she refused to examine too deeply, she felt awkward and tongue-tied in his presence and her heart had an annoying habit of beating a little faster whenever she caught a glimpse of him.

She knew that she had been allocated to the clinic because the nursing staff were very experienced. If she was honest, there wasn't much they couldn't do, and essentially Kirsty was simply another pair of hands. They remained fantastically patient with her and she was learning so much. She hadn't dreamed how much the work would absorb her. There was so much she needed to know, and she found herself furiously reading up on tropical diseases every night after work. She was determined to learn so she could be a real help to her patients and the staff.

Everybody was going out of their way to make her feel supported and every day her admiration grew for all her colleagues who gave so much of themselves to their work. Her life back in the UK seemed shallow by comparison. The thought that she had almost married Robbie dismayed her now. If she had, she would never have known what else life had to offer.

Earlier that day there had been another nasty road accident, with multiple casualties, and all the other doctors were in Theatre, dealing with the aftermath. Once again Kirsty's offer of help was politely but firmly rejected.

'We get one of these most weeks,' Greg said. 'If we stopped the clinic and pulled all the medical staff in every time, the queue at Outpatients would become unmanageable. And as I am sure you are aware, they need to be treated just as urgently as our accident victims.'

'I'd like to assist some time,' Kirsty protested. 'With the way staffing is here, there are bound to be times, especially at night, when you'll need me in Theatre.' So far Kirsty had not been allowed to be on call at night. The others continued to cover it between them.

Greg rubbed a tired hand over his face. He works too hard, Kirsty thought. They all do.

'I know this isn't a teaching hospital, Greg, but you're going to have to let me do my share of nights on call sooner or later. And the more I've assisted, the better prepared I'll be.'

Greg eyed her thoughtfully. 'You're right. It's simply that I wanted to give you enough time to ease yourself in gently before putting you on nights. As you know, Kirsty, we don't have the luxury of staffing that would let us give you the next morning off to catch up on sleep. You would still have to do a full day's work in Outpatients the next day, regardless of how much sleep you'd had. And as I've told you before, an inexperienced doctor is one thing, but an inexperienced and exhausted doctor is another matter all together.'

Kirsty felt inordinately disappointed and not a little indignant at his words. Clearly, as yet, she had not convinced him that she could cope.

'There you go again,' she said crossly. 'Treating me like a child. What about if I do on-call with one of you? I can shadow you, be another pair of hands. That way you'll see I'm tougher than I look. You're on tomorrow night—I could do it with you. I'm not scheduled to work on Saturday or Sunday, so I'll have plenty of time to recover.' She was determined to get her way.

'Actually, I was going to speak to you about that. Sarah and Jamie are covering the weekend and have insisted that Jenny and I take some time off from the hospital. You see…' he smiled tiredly '…you're not the only one who gets ordered about.' He looked rueful and Kirsty could tell from his expression that there must have been quite a battle. Having spent some time with Sarah, she knew that her colleague could be a force to be reckoned with. Nevertheless, she guessed Jamie had backed up his wife if they had managed to persuade Greg to take time off. She smiled to herself at the thought of Greg getting as good as he gave for once. It was a distinctly pleasant image—let him feel what it was like to be bullied.

'Anyway,' Greg went on, 'Jenny is determined that she and I visit one of the nearby national parks and has suggested you come along too. She says it might be some time before you get the opportunity again, especially once you take your share of being on call.' He raised an eyebrow at her little smile of satisfaction. 'But perhaps you'd rather go to the city for the weekend. Do some shopping? Go to a restaurant, take in a movie? A couple of the nursing staff are going to see family and would, I'm sure, be delighted to give you a lift.'

'I hadn't planned to do anything this weekend,' Kirsty said, 'except possibly more studying. And as for going to the city to shop, spending money on clothes seems impossible under the circumstances.' In fact, Kirsty had given away quite a few of her possessions to some of the patients. There had been more than one young woman who had left with one of Kirsty's favourite brightly coloured scarves or even a T-shirt or skirt. She loved seeing the delight on their faces, even though in the greater scheme of things it was such a small gesture on her part. The women often exclaimed over her hair. The nursing staff explained that most of them had never seen a redhead before. Kirsty was growing accustomed to their curiosity and the fact that the patients liked touching her hair.

'But I'd love to see more of the country,' she went on. 'I've never been to a game reserve before. If you're sure Sarah and Jamie won't need the extra help and you wouldn't mind me coming along. I wouldn't like to intrude.'

'That's settled, then,' Greg said. 'We'll leave on Saturday after the clinic and rounds. It's only about an hour's drive away, so we'll be there in plenty of time to do some evening game viewing. I'm warning you, though,' he cautioned, 'this isn't one of the luxury camps you might have read about. This one's pretty basic. Tents rather than cabins.' Before Kirsty could protest that he was once again talking to her as if she were some kind of spoilt rich kid, he went on, 'I must go. I can hear the ambulances in the distance.' And with that he turned on his heel and left.

Two hours later when Kirsty thought she had seen the last patient of the day, Bounty, one of the nurses, came to her looking perplexed. 'There's another patient for you. He's just turned up. He has come far. Usually at this time I'd send him to our emergency department, but none of the doctors are available. They're all still in Theatre.'

'That's all right, Bounty,' Kirsty said. 'I'm quite happy to see him.'

'I'll bring him in, then,' she said. 'I don't know what can be wrong with him. And if I don't know…' She didn't need to finish her sentence. Kirsty knew what she meant. If the highly experienced nurses didn't know what was wrong, it was unlikely Kirsty would know either. Regardless, Kirsty thought defiantly, she would make her own assessment. If, after that, she couldn't make a diagnosis, then she would call in the troops.

Moments later Bounty ushered in a gaunt-looking man of about forty. His breathing was laboured and Kirsty could see from the dusky hue to his lips that he was struggling to take in enough oxygen. Briefly Bounty filled Kirsty in on the history.

'According to the patient, the breathlessness

came on quite suddenly. There's no history of heart or lung problems.' Her brow crinkled. 'His blood pressure is only 70 over 30.'

Kirsty felt a surge of adrenaline. She had to do something—and quickly. He was in imminent danger of collapse, so there was no time to wait for help. She examined him quickly but thoroughly. 'Right, A,B,C,' she told herself. 'Airway, breathing, circulation.' His airway was clear, with nothing obvious causing the breathing difficulties, but there was something odd about his pulse. Every time he gasped for breath, his pulse almost seemed to disappear. Suddenly Kirsty knew exactly what was the matter with her patient.

'It's cardiac tamponade. It's quite rare, so you won't see it very often. But I saw it when I was on a surgical rotation. It fits the pattern. I'm going to have to insert a needle to drain the fluid around his heart.' Kirsty was pleased that this time she was going to be able to teach the nurses something. For once she was going to be of real help.

Quickly Kirsty made her preparations. She

asked Bounty to explain to the patient what she was going to do. Taking a breath to steady herself—she needed to be very precise—she directed the needle upwards from his stomach towards his heart with one single movement. Just as the needle pierced the skin, Greg threw open the door to the treatment room.

'What the hell are you doing?' Although his voice was calm and level, Kirsty could see from the expression in his narrowed blue eyes that he was alarmed. Alarmed and angry. 'I thought I told you to call me if there was anything—'

'We tried to call you. You were tied up in Theatre. Besides, I knew what I needed to do and there was no time to waste.' As she talked, she drew back on the plunger and straw-coloured fluid filled the syringe. Almost immediately the patient's breathing improved and his lips lost their bluish tinge. She emptied the first syringe and filled another before withdrawing it from the chest. As Greg watched in silence, Kirsty turned to the nurse. 'The fluid has been building up around his heart, stopping it from pumping properly. That's why he's been so breathless and his blood pressure low. Now we need to find out what caused it in the first place. Could you send this to the lab for cytology and culture, please?'

'I see I underestimated you,' Greg said finally. 'That was an inspired diagnosis. How did you know?'

'I do know a bit of medicine,' Kirsty responded tartly, before relaxing and grinning broadly. She couldn't quite manage to disguise how pleased she felt with herself. 'Actually, I saw a case like this fairly recently. Pretty impressive, huh?' She blushed, realising that her words could be misconstrued. 'I mean the procedure and the outcome, not me.'

'I think the doctor was pretty impressive, too,' Greg said quietly. 'Never refuse to take credit for a job well done. Maybe there is more of your father in you than you realise, girl.'

Girl? What did he mean, *girl?* He was at it again. Patronising her. Making her feel too young as well as too inexperienced. And what was that remark about her father supposed to mean? Hadn't she made it clear that the last thing she wanted was to be compared with him?

Hadn't Greg understood what she had been saying on the drive back from the village?

'Anyway…' she went on, biting down on her anger. She wouldn't let him see that he had infuriated her. Not until she got what she wanted, at any rate. 'Does that mean you'll let me do my share of on-call now?'

Greg laughed. 'OK, you win. You can do tomorrow night with me. On condition that you call me if there's anything at all you're unsure of. And, yes, if there is a case that needs to go to Theatre, you can assist.'

'How very gracious of you.' This time Kirsty couldn't keep the sarcasm from her voice.

'I am trying to protect you as well as the patients, Dr Boucher. This isn't personal, no matter what you think. I'm sure that in a short time you'll be managing fine on your own—most of the time.' Kirsty knew there was little point in arguing. She would just have to continue to prove herself. In time she would make him revise his opinion of her. She couldn't wait to see the mighty Dr du Toit eat his words.

CHAPTER SEVEN

THE next day the whole team managed to gather in the staffroom for lunch. Kirsty was beginning to realise what a rare event this was. The sheer numbers of patients meant that there was always someone in Theatre or on the wards, but today everyone had made it for lunch at the same time and there was almost a party atmosphere.

'I gather you've been enticed away by Jenny and Greg for an overnight stay at Pelindaba Game Park,' Sarah said. 'Lucky you. Jamie and I took Calum there once, but he kept squealing with excitement every time we got close to the animals and frightened them away.' She laughed. 'We didn't make ourselves too popular with the rest of the group. I think we'll have to wait until he's a bit older before we go again.'

'Or perhaps leave him with Sibongele,' Jamie

said pointedly. 'It would be nice to get away, just the two of us.'

'He's a bit young yet, Jamie. Not that I don't trust Sibo, but it would be unfair to burden him when he has so much on his plate already,' Sarah protested, and from the looks on their faces Kirsty suspected that this was a discussion that they'd had before. It seemed as if Sarah couldn't bear to be parted from her child, even for a short time.

'I could look after him some time if you'd like,' Kirsty offered.

Sarah looked at her speculatively. 'No offence, Kirsty, but you don't strike me as the kind of woman who has had much experience looking after young children.'

'Well, that's where you'd be wrong,' Greg interjected quietly. Kirsty hadn't even been aware that he'd been listening. 'I've seen her in action with a child, a very frightened and bewildered boy, and she worked miracles with him. I think if you ever left Calum in Kirsty's hands, they would be safe hands indeed.'

Everyone looked at Greg, surprised at his support of Kirsty.

But no one could have been more surprised than Kirsty herself.

'Do you come from a large family, then?' Sarah asked.

Kirsty felt uncomfortably aware that everyone had stopped talking and were now regarding her with interest.

'I'm an only child,' Kirsty said. At least, she was now. 'But I worked at a children's hospice during the university holidays and my last rotation before coming here was in paediatrics. The children seemed to take to me—perhaps it was because I didn't talk down to them.' Kirsty couldn't help slide a pointed glance in Greg's direction. But he seemed oblivious to her hidden meaning.

'Oh, well, perhaps we will take you up on your offer soon. Once Calum has got used to you,' Sarah conceded, earning Kirsty a warm smile from Jamie.

'And we'd all chip in, wouldn't we, Greg?' Jenny added. 'You know I would have offered, Sarah, but as much as I love Calum I'm simply not the maternal type. Never wanted children, and it's probably just as well I never had them. The kids here are more than enough for me.'

'What about you, Kirsty? Do you want children?' Jenny asked

'Yes. Not for a while, but eventually.' Kirsty desperately wanted to steer the conversation away from herself. As much as she liked and trusted her colleagues, she wasn't prepared yet to go into her private life. What she had told Greg had been an aberration, but she felt certain he wouldn't have repeated her confidences.

As if sensing her discomfort, Greg changed the subject.

'I think Kirsty will enjoy the game reserve,' he said. 'I have warned her that it's pretty basic.'

'And pretty close to the wildlife,' Jamie added. 'At night it feels as if you are right in the thick of things. When we were there Sarah was certain a lion was about to have us for supper. She almost made me pack up and leave there and then.'

'I wouldn't have minded so much being eaten as long as you were too, sweetheart, but the thought of Calum being some wild animal's aperitif was a bit much.' Sarah slid a mischievous look Jamie's way.

'It's perfectly safe,' Jenny interjected. 'There is no way the animals can get to you. They're on the other side of an electric fence. It only sounds as if they are close by. It's wonderful,' she continued. 'You really feel part of the bush.'

'Oh, I don't think Kirsty would be frightened of a lion,' Greg said. 'I have a suspicion her fears lie in another direction.' Kirsty shot him a withering look, daring him to go on. But it seemed as if Greg had no intention of sharing her secret. 'I suspect it's the lack of creature comforts that will scare Kirsty off,' he went on, just as she was beginning to feel benevolent towards him.

'I don't know where you get this idea I'm unable to tolerate a bit of discomfort,' Kirsty countered. 'I was in the Guides. And we went camping once.' She didn't add that it had been the camping that had finished the Guides for her, and that after only a couple of weeks. What anyone ever saw in camping was beyond her. Give her a comfy bed, a plasma TV and top-quality toiletries. Add in a spa—now, that was bliss. Or it had been once. Lately she wasn't at all sure if the new Kirsty would find the experience quite as enjoyable as she would once have done. But, still, a tent!

'Does it have to be a tent?' Kirsty said. 'Isn't there anything available that is slightly more upmarket? Even a simple cabin would do me— as long as there was a bed.'

'Don't worry, Kirsty.' Jenny laughed. 'These are tents but not as you know them. They have camp beds and small fridges. There is even a separate bedroom for the two of us. Greg will make do in the main area. They are just like mini-homes. Trust me, you'll find them perfectly adequate.'

'Oh, are we in one tent, then?' Kirsty asked. For some reason the thought of having Greg sleeping under the same roof dismayed her. But, she reassured herself, Jenny would be there.

'They are very spacious. You'll see,' Jenny said, standing. 'Come on, guys, we'd better get moving. Theatre starts in ten. I gather you're to assist Greg with the list this afternoon, Kirsty?'

It was the first Kirsty had heard of it, but at Greg's nod she realised that she must have finally passed some sort of test. 'You'll need as much experience of operating as possible if you are to start doing your own on-call in a couple of weeks,' he said. 'And from what I've seen so far, you're a pretty fast learner.' Kirsty felt her heart lift. It seemed that at last she was being given the chance to prove herself. Surgery was where she had hoped to specialise and although she loved Outpatients, operating was where her heart was.

The afternoon passed quickly. Kirsty found Theatre every bit as interesting as she had hoped.

Her first patient was a woman at full term of pregnancy. She had four children already, the last two delivered by Caesarean section.

'I thought you didn't believe in doing Caesars on the women out here,' Kirsty said as she and Greg scrubbed up.

'I only don't believe in inappropriate Caesars. However, because the patient has had two previously there is a very real danger of her rupturing her uterus if we attempt to let her deliver normally. Happily she has attended the hospital regularly, so we have been able to monitor her closely. She has also decided to have her tubes tied while we are at it. She's content with the size of her family and doesn't want to risk another pregnancy. If you do the section, I'll do the sterilisation and you can assist. Are you OK with that?'

Kirsty nodded. Immediately before her paediatric rotation she had spent six months in surgery. Her consultant had been a patient teacher, happy to let her assist in as many cases as she was able to. Still, this would be the first time she would actually be the primary surgeon.

'Wouldn't you prefer to do it? And I can assist?' Kirsty said, the responsibility suddenly hitting causing her new-found confidence to desert her again.

'You'll be fine doing the op,' Greg said. 'I'll be right beside you, watching you every step of the way. Don't worry, by the time you leave here you'll be able to do them in your sleep. The more practice you get now, the better. There is a good chance that you may find yourself in a position where you are the only person available to do one in an emergency, so it's best you get as much experience in a controlled situation—where one of us is around to help you out if need be. But, if you'd rather not, that's OK, too.' Greg lifted an eyebrow in question. Kirsty knew that a gauntlet had been thrown down. She had been asking him repeatedly to give her more responsibility. Now she needed to show him that she was ready. And she knew what to do. Silently, she pulled on her face mask and held out her hand for a scalpel.

Greg said very little as she operated on the woman, just watched carefully, ready to step in if Kirsty showed any signs of faltering. But she didn't need his help, although his presence gave her confidence. She took her time and was pleased with the result. Once the baby had been delivered, a healthy boy who had disrupted the quiet of the theatre with his gusty cries, she had swapped sides with Greg and assisted as he had quickly and efficiently tied the woman's tubes. His right hand had shown no indication of being unable to manipulate the scalpel.

As if reading her thoughts, Greg said, 'I used to be a neurosurgeon, but the damage to my hand put paid to intricate brain surgery. Most days my hand is fine, but some days it stiffens up. On good days, which, thank God, are most days, I can still operate, but I leave the very fine or delicate stuff to Jamie. And obviously brain surgery is out of the question. Not that we'd do that here anyway, except if we had no choice in an emergency. We really don't have the facilities.'

'He was one of the best neurosurgeons in the country, and well on his way to gaining an international reputation,' Jenny said from her position at the top of the table, where she was monitoring the patient's vital signs. 'Still, their loss is our gain.'

Greg looked at Jenny. Above his mask his eyes glittered. 'Jenny exaggerates,' he said. 'However, the teaching hospital where I learned offered some of the best experience in the world in the field. I was very fortunate to have the opportunity to train there.'

Despite the even tone, Kirsty knew it must have been a blow for Greg. Not only had the fire cost him his family, but it seemed it had cost him his career, too.

'You miss it?' Kirsty asked.

Blue eyes turned in her direction. They seemed to drill right through her.

'My life is here now,' he said. He stood aside. 'Would you like to close?'

Kirsty finished stitching the wound in the woman's abdomen before standing back to admire her handiwork.

'You have very neat hands,' Greg said approvingly. 'It seems, Jenny, that we have a surgeon in the making here.'

Kirsty felt a warm glow at his praise. Whatever else she thought of him, he was generous when it came to praise. However, she suspected he'd be equally unstinting with his criticism if he thought it would make her a better doctor. She hoped that she wouldn't find out.

After they finished the list, Kirsty slipped away to check on her first patient. She found the mother in the maternity ward fully conscious and her baby suckling contentedly. Kirsty peered into the blanket, catching a glimpse of long eyelashes that lay against chubby cheeks the colour of dark chocolate. She felt a twinge of longing. She wondered if she would ever know the joy of motherhood. To have children, be a part of a large, happy family. To love and be loved in return. Unconditionally. For herself. She had once thought that was to be part of her future, now she wondered if it was ever meant to be.

Greg had insisted that she take a couple of hours off before making herself available to share the on-call.

'We might be quiet,' he said, 'although, being a Friday night, we do tend to get our share of road accidents and one or two stabbings. As it's your first night, Jenny is going to be second on call. That way we won't have to disturb either Sarah or Jamie if things get busy. They need as much rest as possible before the weekend. And you should get some rest, too, while you can. You're off until nine. After that I'll call you if I need you.'

'What about you?' Kirsty asked. 'When will you get some rest? You've been up since the crack of dawn,'

'I'll have a run then a swim. That's usually enough to recharge my batteries. I find I don't need much sleep.' He stretched and his top rode up, offering Kirsty a tantalising glimpse of his bronzed abdomen. Her stomach flipped. She had a brief memory of him in her bed, his arms circling her waist and his hands on her bare arms, his breath on her face. She couldn't stop herself imagining running her hands over his abdomen, up to his chest, pulling him close.

She shut her eyes in case he read her thoughts. What *was* she thinking? What was it about this man that made her think this way? She had never experienced pure animal attraction before. Had thought it was impossible. How could you lust after someone when you didn't really like them? But, she realised, she was beginning to like Greg du Toit. She was beginning to like him very much indeed.

'OK, I'm off. Enjoy your swim, run— whatever. I'm away for a shower and a nap. Actually, I might pop over and see Sarah and Calum for a bit first. He is so adorable. And I should let him get to know me in case Sarah and Jamie take me up on my offer of babysitting. I know Jamie would love to have a couple of days with Sarah.' God, now she was babbling. Greg was looking at her as if she were slightly deranged. Kirsty decided that removing herself from his company until she got her wayward thoughts back under control—if she could get them back under control—was by far the most sensible course of action. 'So I'm off,' she repeated, pointing in the vague direction of her house. As Greg's look of confusion deepened, she turned and walked away.

'And don't forget to have something to eat,' Greg shouted after her retreating back. 'I don't want you collapsing with hunger on me through the night because you haven't consumed enough calories.'

Kirsty felt her spine stiffen. There he went again. He really was the most patronising, old-fashioned, sexist man she had ever met. She couldn't imagine him talking to one of the male doctors like that. Maybe she didn't like him so much after all.

Kirsty sat drinking a cup of coffee in Sarah's house. She had showered and tried to nap, but she hadn't been able to relax enough to sleep. So in the end she had decided to do what she had told Greg she might do—go and see Sarah. Perhaps the company of another woman would bring her back to reality.

Calum had been a ball of energy as he'd torn around the house, dragging Kirsty after him. He'd seemed determined to point out every last toy and item of furniture in the house. Sarah had watched fondly with her feet up.

'Thank God you came!' she exclaimed. 'This seems to be a new game. I've been around the house five times this afternoon, trying to explain why a chair is called a chair. Actually, he's learning a few words from Sophie, who looks after him when I'm at work. I'll probably end up learning more of the language from him than from the tapes and books I bought. Never seem to find a spare moment to look at the wretched things.'

'Can I borrow them for a bit, then?' Kirsty asked eagerly. 'I really want to learn, too.'

'Be my guest.' Sarah waved tiredly at the pile of books that lay in a haphazard heap on the coffee-table. 'If you take them, at least I won't have to feel guilty every time I look at them.

'How are things going anyway?' Sarah asked.

'Finding your feet? I hear you've done some great work—with outpatients and in Theatre.'

'Thanks,' Kirsty said with a smile. 'Everyone's been fantastic. Making me feel part of the team. There to offer advice and help when I need it. Particularly Greg.' Kirsty laughed ruefully. 'Although he's been mostly very positive, I'm not so sure he's convinced I'm up to it yet.'

'Greg's a hard taskmaster,' Sarah said slowly, 'but when it comes to making sure the patients receive the best possible care, he doesn't allow personal feelings to get in the way.'

'That's just it,' Kirsty said. 'I'm not sure that he *approves* of me. I still wonder if he'd be happier if I wasn't here—if I gave up, packed my bags and went home, tail between my legs.'

Sarah looked at Kirsty keenly. 'Do you think so? I hadn't got that impression at all. I get the feeling that our Greg is getting used to having you around.'

Before Kirsty had time to consider Sarah's words there was a loud crash from the kitchen, followed by wails of outrage. They both jumped to their feet and ran into the kitchen to find Calum sitting on the floor, surrounded by pots and pans. Despite his cries, he was clearly uninjured. Sarah picked him up and calmed him down with soothing words.

'Fell on me,' Calum whimpered.

'Pulled them on top of yourself more like, young man,' Sarah said, 'but you're all right now.' She glanced at Kirsty with a rueful smile. 'Being the mother of a toddler, you need eyes in the back of your head.' She kissed Calum until his tears were replaced with squeals of laughter.

'Does this little monster put you off having children?' Sarah asked Kirsty over the top of Calum's head.

'No, I want children,' Kirsty said quietly. 'But first I have to find the right man.'

'No one serious in your life, then?' Sarah asked, setting Calum back down. 'I'll need to get you ready for bed in a moment.'

'There was…' Kirsty hesitated. 'Once. But, no, no one at the moment.'

Sarah looked at her quizzically, inviting her to go on.

'A month ago I was engaged. I should be on

my honeymoon right now,' she admitted, straining to keep the bitterness from her voice.

'Do you want to tell me about it?' Sarah asked softly.

'There's nothing much to tell. Robbie and I went out for years. I met him when he started working with my father. We seemed to have a lot in common. We both enjoyed the same things—the theatre, restaurants, clubbing. Last year we got engaged. At the time it seemed the right thing to do, the inevitable next step. I thought I had my life mapped out. A career I love, a life with the man I loved, children in the future…' She tailed off.

'What went wrong?' Sarah prompted.

'I found him in bed with someone a couple of weeks before the wedding. My wedding day was supposed to be the day I arrived here.'

'Sounds like you're better off without him. But you must have been deeply hurt,' Sarah said sympathetically.

'I was—at first. Now I'm just angry and, I have to admit, relieved. It wasn't just the fact he had been sleeping with someone else—what really made me furious was that I had agreed that we wouldn't have children. He didn't want them. Told me that we didn't need them in our lives. Of course, I hoped that eventually I would be able to change his mind, but I *was* prepared to give up my dreams for him. For a man who couldn't even be faithful to me. How stupid was that?'

'You can't blame yourself, Kirsty. Just be glad you found out that he was a snake before you got married.'

'I wonder now if I ever really loved him,' Kirsty said slowly. 'It's only been a few weeks, but I don't miss him at all. Now all I can think about is how close I came to making the worst mistake of my life. I suspect that all along he was only using me; that he thought marriage to me would cement his position in my father's private practice. It's worth an awful lot of money.'

'Is that the real reason you came out here, then? Running away from a broken love affair?' Sarah held up her hands as Kirsty started to protest. 'Don't worry, I don't blame you. Whatever your reasons for coming out here, it's clear to us that you are prepared to work hard and to learn. At the end of the day, that's what matters.'

'I'm not sure Greg would share your view,' Kirsty said. 'I suspect if he knew why I came here, he'd believe his initial assumptions about me were right. And although it may have been the reason I came initially, it's not why I'm staying. So, please, Sarah, don't tell him.'

Sarah looked at Kirsty, a small frown creasing her brow. 'His good opinion matters to you, doesn't it?' she said. 'Be careful that you don't allow it to matter too much.'

'What do you mean?' Kirsty replied defensively. 'Of course I want Greg to think well of me professionally. That's all.' But she could see from Sarah's expression that she wasn't convinced. 'Believe me, Sarah,' she went on, 'I have no aspirations in any other direction.' She laughed shakily, knowing as she said the words that they weren't quite true. Greg's good opinion did matter. It mattered much more than Kirsty wanted to admit. Even to herself. She stood up. Suddenly she needed to be on her own.

'I should leave you to it,' she said. 'I'm on call tonight, so I need to try and get some rest.'

'And I'll need to get this young man ready for

bed,' Sarah yawned. 'I'm pretty well ready for bed myself. Enjoy your weekend if I don't see you. Try and force Greg to relax. That man could do with some rest and recuperation.'

Make Greg relax? Kirsty thought. She couldn't imagine anything more difficult. The man was a like a coiled spring and she couldn't imagine him being any other way.

The night on call went smoothly. Kirsty spent the first part of the evening accompanying Greg on his rounds.

'We'll start in Paeds,' Greg said. 'There are a couple of patients there I want to see.'

As they entered the ward Kirsty was struck afresh at the drabness of it. The paediatric wards back home had been stuffed with toys, televisions and mobiles. There were always plenty of nursing staff and even play leaders to keep the children occupied. But here it was a different story. The ward was empty except for the rows of cots, some with two children in each. With only two nurses on duty, most of the children lay quietly, looking up at a bare ceiling. With the exception of three or four children whose mothers comforted them or lay sleeping on the floor next to their cots, there was no one free to offer the children the cuddles and attention they needed. Kirsty thought her heart would break as she looked down at the innocent faces that gazed up at her not expecting comfort. There was one child in particular who had kicked off his blanket, his cries of distress unheeded. To her surprise, Greg scooped the wailing infant up into his arms as he passed the cot and carried the child across to the nurses' station. As he talked to the nurses he rocked the child absent-mindedly until his sobs turned to whimpers and then his eyes closed in sleep. Still carrying the sleeping child, Greg accompanied the nursing staff to another cot where a toddler lay semi-conscious, oblivious to the tubes that snaked out from its tiny limbs.

'This child has pneumonia,' Greg told Kirsty. 'As you can see, she's on IV antibiotics and oxygen. However, she's not responding as well as we hoped. Any suggestions?'

'HIV?'

'No. We've tested her and she's negative.'

'TB? Malnutrition? Has she had a skin test? Have the rest of the family been checked? Could also be unrecognised heart disease.'

'Good thinking. I'll leave you to sort that out.'

The next child they went to check was the child from the village, Mathew.

'He's doing well,' Greg said. 'His burns on his arms are getting better, but we won't be sure for some time how much function he'll have retained in his hand. The burns to his face are also healing. Unfortunately, given the infection, there is likely to be scarring. Again we won't know the full extent until the scars have healed completely. But you'll be pleased to hear he has some movement back in his hand.'

'I heard. Sister Matabele told me movement came back when he was in the ambulance.'

Greg looked at her quizzically.

'What? You didn't think I wouldn't go and find out as soon as I could? Anyway what next?' Kirsty asked. 'Plastic surgery?'

Greg smiled ruefully. 'I wish. There is no way this child's parents will be able to afford remedial surgery for their child. They can barely afford food, never mind anything else. No, I'm afraid the best they can hope for is their son returned in one piece with full use of his limbs.'

Once again Kirsty felt outraged and then ashamed. Before coming here she hadn't really given much thought to the privileged life she had been living. As a child she had wanted for nothing, apart from her father's attention perhaps, and as an adult she had never thought twice about how she had spent her money. But if these children didn't have material possessions, at least some of them had their parents' love.

'Where are the parents of the other children?' she demanded. 'I know the nursing staff are too short-handed to play with the children, but what about the families? Surely it can't be good for them not to be with their children at a time like this?'

Greg looked around the ward. 'Most of these children don't have parents. The HIV/AIDS virus has wiped out a large proportion of the adult population in this region. Almost all of the children here are here because they are suffering the consequences of the infection. We didn't get the drugs in time to help the parents but hopefully, with the increase in funding available for retroviral drugs for children, most of these children will lead long, healthy lives.'

'What? In an orphanage? Without parents? Not good enough.'

'No, it's not.' He looked around. 'You're right to be angry. I guess we've become slightly inured to it. We do what we can, but it's not nearly enough. Sarah and Jamie buy toys for the children, but the children take them with them when they leave. Most of them have never had a shop-bought toy. We all wish we had money to do more. We need more staff, better facilities, more drugs.' He stooped down to replace the sleeping infant in his arms back in his cot, covering him with a blanket. 'I go along to local meetings to try and raise more money, and we have been successful to a degree. We have a lot more equipment and drugs than there were when we first arrived, but we could always do with more. In the meantime, until we can get more, we prioritise.'

'Still not enough,' Kirsty repeated.

'I know. In the meantime, as I said before, we do what we can. We try and keep an emotional distance. We can't get too involved with our patients. We need to remain objective so we can treat them as best we can.'

'Emotional distance. Huh,' Kirsty retorted. 'And how much emotional distance did you feel towards that child you just held in your arms?'

Greg frowned and Kirsty could see she had scored a point. Greg was always going on about not getting involved with the patients, but she could see, and not just from the way he had held the child, that the fate of the children touched him deeply. Perhaps the macho Dr du Toit wasn't as good at keeping his emotional distance as he thought. And as for Sarah and Jamie, they were fostering one of the children!

'That doesn't count. I had a free pair of arms. And now, Dr Boucher, shall we move on?'

A couple of hours later they finished their rounds. There were a few patients who would require monitoring through the night, but apart from that, and some minor injuries requiring suturing, the hospital was quiet. Greg suggested they go back to staff quarters once they had finished seeing to the patients.

They found Jenny there, reading a paper. She looked up as they entered.

'Hi, you two. I was hoping you'd be back here before I went to bed.'

'Why? What's up?' Greg asked settling himself down on one of the sofas, indicating to Kirsty with a sweep of his hand that she should do the same.

'I'm afraid I'm going to have to call off tomorrow,' Jenny said, regret evident in her voice. 'I've had a call from a close friend who is having some sort of personal crisis, and I think I need to go and see her tomorrow instead of going on our trip.'

'No problem,' said Greg. 'We'll reschedule for another time.'

Kirsty was dismayed at how disappointed she felt. She hadn't appreciated how much she had been looking forward to going away. And she had to admit it wasn't just disappointment at missing out on seeing more of the country.

'Oh, you two must still go,' Jenny said.

'Heavens knows when the opportunity will come your way again.'

'If you're not going—' Kirsty began.

Jenny cut her short. 'It was difficult enough to get Greg to agree to go in the first place,' she said to Kirsty, 'so don't back out now because I can't go, or he'll never take time off.'

'I don't need time off,' Greg protested. 'And, anyway, I've been to this particular camp at least twice so I don't need to go again.'

'Ah, but Kirsty hasn't been. I'm sure she's been looking forward to it. Think of your staff,' Jenny admonished. 'They need to get a break even if you don't.'

'Don't worry about me,' Kirsty interrupted hastily. 'I'm sure there'll be plenty of other opportunities for us all to go.' The realisation of what Jenny was suggesting was beginning to sink in. The thought of spending the best part of a weekend alone with Greg was disconcerting, to say the least. As far as Kirsty was concerned, there was safety in numbers.

'You see, Kirsty doesn't want to go either,' Greg said—with an undue amount of satisfaction, she thought. It appeared as if he were no more keen to spend time alone with her than she was with him.

'You listen to me, young man,' Jenny said, drawing herself up to her full five feet two inches. 'Everyone needs a break—even supermen like yourself. You'll go as planned and take this young lady with you. Otherwise I'll be forced to ring my friend and tell her I can't make it after all. And that will make me feel bad. And you don't want that, do you?' Jenny wiggled an eyebrow at Greg. Despite her slight smile, Kirsty could tell she meant every word. And clearly Greg did, too. He laughed before holding his hands up in mock surrender.

'See what I have to put up with. Just because Jenny has known me since I was a kid, she thinks she can boss me around.'

'Well, someone needs to,' Jenny retorted. 'For your own good. Now, can I assume that's settled? You and Kirsty will go as planned?'

'OK, OK. You win—if you can persuade Kirsty, that is. You may well find that there are a thousand things she'd rather do than spend time with her boss.'

While Kirsty was searching for an excuse that would let Greg off the hook, she felt the full force of Jenny's severe look turned on her.

'No, no, I would love to go,' she found herself saying. 'I mean, if Greg doesn't mind.'

She was rewarded by a warm smile from Jenny. 'That's settled, then. I don't want to hear any more about it. If I come back and find the trip was cancelled...' she wagged a finger at them both '...there will be hell to pay. Do I make myself clear?'

'Yes, ma'am,' Greg and Kirsty said simultaneously. They shared a smile. It seemed as if there was no backing out for either of them. Kirsty was amused to see Greg find himself outmanoeuvred by his older colleague. Before this evening, she would never have guessed that anyone would have been able to make him do anything he didn't want to do.

After Jenny left, Greg yawned and turned to Kirsty. 'Why don't you go home? It's pretty quiet. I'll call you if anything comes in.'

'I'm happy to stay.'

'There's no need. I'm going back to my house.

They'll call me there if they need me. Do you want to hang about here on your own?'

'I might as well go home, too, then,' Kirsty said reluctantly. 'But you promise to call me?'

'I promise,' Greg said. 'But don't be surprised if there's no need. I know you'll find this hard to believe, we do sometimes get a quiet night. And the nurses are used to coping with most things.' He stood up. 'Come on. I'll walk you back.'

Once she was back in her own place, Kirsty found herself too restless to sleep. The image of the children in the ward kept coming back to haunt her. She couldn't accept that there was nothing to be done about the ward or that there was nothing to be done about Mathew's face. Slowly an idea was beginning to form in the back of her mind. No, she tried to dismiss the thought. She couldn't ask. He had never helped her before, so why would he agree to do so now? But the idea wouldn't go away. It was, she thought, at least worth a try. Making up her mind, she crossed over to her rickety dressing-table, pulled out some writing paper from one of the drawers and sat down and wrote a letter.

CHAPTER EIGHT

SHE hadn't been called by anyone through the night, and when Kirsty arrived on the wards shortly after sunrise, Greg had already finished rounds.

'I promise, there was no reason to call you,' Greg said before Kirsty could berate him. 'And because we were quiet, I though I'd make an early start on rounds so we can leave in plenty of time to get to the camp before sundown.'

'I'm not sure I believe you, but it's too late now. I'll just make a start in Outpatients, shall I?' Even though it was still early on a Saturday morning, Kirsty knew that there would already be a queue of patients waiting to see her.

'I'll come and help as soon as I'm done here,' Greg said.

'I can manage fine on my own,' Kirsty said stiffly.

'Don't be so prickly, woman. I'm sure you'll

manage fine. But two pairs of hands are better than one. And the sooner we finish, the sooner we can leave. Now I'm committed to going, I'm quite looking forward to it.'

And, sure enough, once Greg arrived to help, the clinic was finished in record time. Kirsty had to admit to herself they made a good team. It was almost as if instinctively each knew what the other was thinking. As far as the patients were concerned, that was.

Once they had finished the clinic and had had lunch, they set off. Kirsty had dressed in a pair of beige shorts and a white T-shirt. She had brushed her hair into a high ponytail to keep her neck cool. Uncertain of what to pack, she had eventually decided on a pair of jeans, a dress, a couple of T-shirts, a skirt, a couple of sweaters and limited herself to three pairs of shoes. Heels, walking boots and sandals. With a swimming costume and a sarong, as well as a couple of novels thrown in for good measure, she considered herself prepared for any eventuality.

Greg, however, had raised an eyebrow when she lugged her case out to his car.

'Good grief, woman, we're only going for a night, unless you're planning to make an early escape back to the UK?'

'I'm not going back. Not until my time is up or you fire me. Accept it,' she responded tartly. 'And, unlike you, I have no idea what one wears on safari, so I've come prepared.'

Greg laughed. 'Lucky there's plenty of space in the boot, then. Come on, let's go.'

As they drove, Greg and Kirsty chatted easily about patients. Kirsty repeated tales of her life as a medical student and as a junior doctor that made Greg laugh.

'I can't believe some of the things we thought.' She smiled. 'We were all so naïve.'

In turn, Greg shared with her some of the difficult cases he'd had to deal with when he'd first arrived. It was clear to Kirsty that, despite the hardships, he found the work immensely rewarding.

'It was just Jenny and I to begin with,' he told Kirsty. 'Until Jamie arrived, we split the workload down the middle.'

'That must have been tough,' Kirsty volunteered. 'Weren't you overwhelmed at all?'

'It was challenging. There's no doubt about that. But Jenny was—still is—a great support. And there was no time for thinking… It wasn't altogether what I did for the hospital. It's what the hospital and the patients did for me. In some ways I think they might have saved my life. Instead of the other way round,' Greg said slowly. 'Hey,' he went on before Kirsty had a chance to respond, 'there's something here I want to show you.' He pulled over to the side of the road. On the left where the veld fell away from the road, Kirsty could see a river.

'Come on,' Greg said, slinging a rucksack over his shoulder, 'it's just down here.'

Kirsty followed Greg for a few hundred yards along the bank. The dry grass of the bush tickled her bare legs.

'There's no snakes here?' she questioned nervously.

'They'll hide when they feel the vibrations from your footsteps. They are only likely to bite if you surprise them. There's not much danger of that.'

When they came to a cluster of sun-bleached

boulders, Greg gestured to Kirsty to sit down. He pulled a bottle of water from a rucksack and passed it to her. As she swallowed she listened to the silence, unbroken except for the swish of the long grass as it moved in the breeze. Greg stayed quiet, although his eyes seemed to be searching the river for something. Suddenly an animal poked its head out of the water with a cry not unlike that of a bull. Its mouth was open, revealing rows of large teeth. Kirsty scampered to her feet, but Greg pulled her back down.

'Don't move,' he ordered.

'What is it?' Kirsty whispered, fascinated.

'A hippo. There's a whole herd that lives in this part of the river.'

'Aren't they supposed to cause more injuries than any other wild animal?' Kirsty asked, not altogether certain she was happy to be in such close proximity to them.

'We're perfectly safe as long as we stay still and keep our distance,' he whispered. 'And, anyway,' he said, reaching into his knapsack and placing a hunting rifle on the ground beside him, 'I have this in case of emergencies.'

Kirsty recoiled. She didn't know which fright-ened her more—the hippo or the gun.

'Is that legal?' she yelped, sliding away from Greg and the weapon.

'Of course. And don't worry. I was brought up on a farm so I know how to use it. Although I have no intention of doing so unless I have to.'

'Well, if you think for one minute that thing is coming anywhere near our tent, you have another think coming.'

'Don't worry. I'll unload it when we get back to the car. The bullets stay locked in the car, the gun stays with me.'

They sat in silence and watched as another two hippos appeared. Kirsty was captivated by their size and quiet presence. If the animals were aware of their audience, they gave no indication of it. After a while they sank below the surface of the water.

'Time to go,' Greg said, unloading the rifle before pulling Kirsty up by the hand.

He held onto her, guiding her around him so that she would be in front as they made their way back to the car. As she squeezed between him and the boulders she stumbled slightly. Greg caught her around the waist, drawing her away from the river. For a moment he held her against him and Kirsty could feel the steady beat of his heart. She looked up to find his eyes locked on hers.

'Careful,' he said huskily, tracing her cheekbone with a long finger. 'You don't want to get hurt.'

The underlying message was clear. Kirsty returned his gaze.

'I'm a grown woman, Greg,' she said. 'You don't have to worry about me. There's no danger of me getting hurt.' But even as she said the words she wondered if they were true. Something told her she was in very real danger indeed.

They arrived at the camp when the sun was still high in the sky, although the heat was beginning to leak from the day. Kirsty was delighted to find that Greg had understated the facilities in the camp. There were tents, but they were perched in the treetops. Theirs had a small balcony with an uninterrupted view of a waterhole. One side had been sectioned off to form a bedroom with a couple of single beds pushed together. In the main part of the tent, there were a couple of chairs, a table and another single bed. Kirsty raised an eyebrow at Greg.

'I guess you won't mind if I have the bedroom?' she said.

'No problem.'

In one corner open to the sky, hidden from view of the other tents, was a shower. Thankfully Kirsty noted it also had a screen to offer privacy from other occupants of the tent. Dumping her bags, she went out onto the balcony. From there she could see that in the centre of the camp was a thatch-roofed structure where they could have a barbeque or sit around a fire with their fellow guests. To one side, just within the perimeter fence, was a small, inviting pool with sun loungers. Kirsty knew where she'd be heading just as soon as she could.

'Isn't this awfully expensive?' she asked Greg as she looked around, the thought tempering her delight somewhat.

'It's not as nearly as expensive as you think and, because the camp is quiet, they've given us an upgrade free. All the profits go back into the upkeep of the reserve and to the villagers, so don't worry, anything we spend here finds its way into the right pockets.'

'In that case, I'm not going to waste a precious minute. I'm off to the pool before the sun goes down. Coming?' Ignoring Greg's astonished look, Kirsty began to remove her T-shirt.

'I was hoping there would be a place for a dip,' she said, 'so I put my costume on underneath my clothes.' And with another brief movement she removed her shorts. Pausing only to grab a towel, she left Greg standing.

Greg stared after Kirsty as she left. He had been taken aback when she had stood in front of him dressed only in the tiniest floral bikini, which emphasised the curve of her breasts, her narrow waist and her abdomen with just the smallest hint of roundness. Her auburn hair contrasted with the alabaster whiteness of her shoulders and, as she turned to leave, he had to admit she had one of the cutest backsides he had seen in a long time.

Despite everything he had been telling himself since Kirsty's arrival, Greg knew with a twist in his guts that he was in trouble. There was no longer any doubt, he was seriously attracted to Kirsty Boucher, and he could think of only one way to get her out of his mind. But an insistent voice needled at his thoughts. It wasn't just a physical attraction. Despite Kirsty's professional inexperience, contrasting with her curious mix of sophistication and vulnerability, Greg was beginning to recognise and admire the determination that underpinned everything she did. It couldn't have been easy for her since she arrived. And, God knew, he hadn't tried to make it easier for her, but she had never complained. Quite the opposite, in fact. She was always asking to do more. He looked down at his hand, twisting the gold band he never removed. He couldn't remember laughing as much in a long time as he had on the journey here. Around Kirsty, he felt happier, more relaxed than he had, well, since Kathleen had died.

The thought made him frown. Not that anyone could ever replace Kathleen. There was no question of that. What he felt for Kirsty was pure animal attraction. That was all. Not for the first time, he regretted agreeing to come here alone with her. It would have been far better, for both their sakes, if there was someone else around. Still, it was too late now. He'd just have to exercise some willpower and he was good at that, wasn't he? Satisfied that he had it all under control, he changed into his swimming shorts and, whistling, went to join Kirsty at the pool.

Greg found Kirsty sitting by the pool. She had grabbed one of the sun loungers, and although the sun had lost most of its heat she was slathering herself in sunscreen. She was attempting to put some on her back but despite her contortions, was failing miserably.

'That's the problem with fair skin,' she muttered to Greg, as he tossed his towel onto the lounger beside her. 'If I don't make sure every inch is covered, I burn so easily.'

'Here, let me,' Greg offered, holding his hand out for the bottle of lotion.

'It's OK, I can manage,' Kirsty said.

'Don't be silly,' Greg responded, taking the bottle from her. 'Turn round and I'll do your back.'

Knowing it would be useless to argue, Kirsty gave in and lay face down on the sun bed. His first touch sent tiny sparks tingling down her spine as his strong hands kneaded her skin. Kirsty buried her face in her towel, lest a low moan of pleasure escaped unbidden from her lips. She couldn't stop herself from imagining his hands roaming all over her body.

'There, that should do.' Greg's voice interrupted her thoughts as he snapped the cap shut on the bottle, bringing her back to earth.

It occurred to her that she should offer to return the favour, but one look at his smooth, tanned skin told her it wasn't necessary. In fact, she thought as she studied him from beneath her lashes, he really had the sexiest physique she had ever seen. She resisted the urge to reach over and run her fingers along his back.

'I think I'll go for a swim,' Kirsty announced. *I could do with cooling off in more ways than one,* she thought.

She felt his eyes on her as she walked to the edge of the pool before diving in. The cool water made her gasp. Within moments, however, her skin had adjusted to the temperature and as she trod water she savoured the coolness of the water on her overheated skin.

'Are you coming in?' she shouted over to Greg.

He shook his head. 'In a while. I'm going to catch up on some reading first.'

He did want to catch up on some reading, Greg thought, but it wasn't just that. He knew he didn't trust himself to be in the water with Kirsty. He opened his book, but found he had no interest in getting back into the complicated plot. Instead, his eyes were drawn back to Kirsty as her slim arms sliced through the water. She certainly was beguiling, he had to admit. But it was nothing more than sexual attraction, he reminded himself as she emerged, dripping, from the pool. Her skimpy bikini clung to her body, emphasising the curve of her breasts, her narrow waist and her long shapely legs. How could he have ever thought she was too thin? She was just right. Greg felt heat low in his abdomen as she padded back to her sun lounger and snatched up her towel.

'I needed that.' She laughed, rubbing her hair. 'But I think I'll go up for a shower.' She looked pointedly at his book, her lips twitching mischievously. 'Leave you to catch up with your reading.'

Greg frowned, wondering what she was finding so amusing, when to his embarrassment he realised he was holding his book upside down.

Kirsty stood under the pounding needles of water, enjoying the novel experience of showering under the sky. When she had finished she dressed in a skirt and T-shirt and unpacked the rest of her clothes.

By the time Greg appeared she was ready.

'I've organised a game viewing. We leave at five in the morning, if that's OK.'

'Sounds good to me.'

'Dinner's at seven. I'm going to take a shower.'

Kirsty stood on the balcony, enchanted to see that a herd of buck and a couple of zebras had come to the waterhole. The sky was a blaze of red as the sun sank in the sky. A faint breeze cooled her skin.

I'm happy, Kirsty thought, surprised. Could it only have been a couple of weeks since she had thought her heart shattered? She wrapped her arms around herself. She couldn't have loved Robbie. Not the way a woman should love the man she planned to spend the rest of her life with. Not if her heart was healing so quickly. She had almost made a terrible mistake. If she had married Robbie, it wouldn't have lasted.

Kirsty was disturbed from her reverie by a distant rumble of thunder. Suddenly she was aware that a bank of dark clouds was rolling in with the night. The air began to fizz with electricity and she shivered as the wind rippled through her skirt.

She felt rather than saw Greg join her on the balcony. He had just stepped out of the shower, a towel wrapped low on his hips and his hair still beaded with waterdrops.

'It looks like a storm's coming,' he said. 'Heaven knows, we can do with the rain.'

Kirsty's gaze was drawn to his broad shoulders, the muscles rippling beneath the skin. Unable to help herself, her eyes took in his narrow waist with the thick trail of dark hairs that led downwards. Feeling a stirring of desire, she turned away abruptly and concentrated on the view.

'Look,' she said, pointing to the waterhole. A herd of elephants was making its slow majestic way to join the zebra and buck, who were already drinking at the water's edge. Unconsciously she held out her hand to Greg. They stood watching the animals for a moment as darkness descended. Kirsty sighed contentedly.

'It's such a magical country.'

Kirsty felt Greg put his arm around her shoulders. Without thinking, she leaned into his body. Suddenly with a muffled curse Greg turned her towards him. He studied her intently, his blue eyes mirroring the stormy sky, before bringing his mouth down on hers.

Kirsty swayed, drowning with desire. She clung to him, returning his kisses with a need that left her breathless. As his kiss deepened he dropped his hands to her hips and pulled her closer. Unable to help herself, her body melted into his as she responded to his touch. She let her hands explore his back, her fingers, as light as feathers, gently tracing the ridges of scars on his body. Suddenly the world was lit up as the sky flashed and another roll of thunder, louder than the one before, rent the air. Greg picked Kirsty up by the waist and she wrapped her legs around his hips. He moaned and his kisses grew ever more insistent as he carried her over to the bed. The room had darkened and Kirsty could barely make out his features as he laid her on top of the sheets. He stood for a moment, his eyes lingering on her body. She reached for him and he lay down beside her. His fingers skimmed over her breasts, tugging at her T-shirt. With trembling hands she assisted him to remove it.

With a swift movement he turned on his back and lifted her onto his hips, where she could feel the strength of his desire. He reached behind her, undoing her bra with one hand, allowing her breasts to spring free before capturing them in a gentle grip. As he explored her body, Kirsty arched her back, soft moans of pleasure escaping from her lips. Her skirt had ridden up and she could feel his hands sweeping over her thighs ever upwards until he found what he was seeking. Wave upon wave of sensation rocked her body until at last he entered her and then she was lost somewhere she had never been.

Afterwards, as they lay in each other's arms, Kirsty knew she had found a place where she felt cherished. Raising herself on one elbow, she traced the scars on Greg's face, following them down across his chest. He circled her wrist with a hand, bringing her fingers to his lips, his other hand gently stroking her shoulder before continuing on to the dip of her waist.

'I didn't know it could be like this,' Kirsty whispered. 'It was never like this with Robbie...' She froze as she realised she had spoken her thoughts out loud.

'Robbie?' Greg asked. His hands stopped their restless exploration of her body.

Kirsty sighed. She didn't want to talk about Robbie right now, but she had no choice. 'My ex-fiancé. We were going to get married. The day I arrived here, in fact. But obviously we didn't—get married, or are ever going to get married.' Grief, she was babbling again. But she needed him to know that it was over between her and Robbie. She looked at Greg, trying to gauge his reaction. But in the dim light his eyes were cool, expressionless.

'I didn't know. I'm sorry,' he said, his voice flat. He hesitated for a moment. 'Tell me about him,' he said quietly.

'There's not much to tell. We met, fell in love—or so I thought. We were going to get married, and then I came home from work early one day. I wanted to surprise him. I surprised him all right.' She couldn't keep the taint of bitterness from her voice. 'In bed with another woman. You know the old cliché. Never thought it would happen to me.'

'Bastard,' Greg said succinctly.

Kirsty laughed. 'I'm beginning to realise it was for the best. He and I disagreed on too many things. We wanted different things from life.'

'Such as?' Greg prodded gently.

'For a start, I wanted children. Oh, not right away, but some time in the future. He didn't.'

'That's a pretty big difference, Kirsty.'

'I thought if I loved him enough, it wouldn't matter. Or that perhaps I could change his mind in time. If he loved *me* enough.'

'A dangerous assumption to make. And now? How do you feel about him? Do you still love him?'

'I'm beginning to realise that I never did truly love him.'

Kirsty laid her head on Greg's chest and continued her exploration of the scars that covered his chest and shoulder with a finger.

'Were you in a lot of pain?' she asked, knowing it wasn't just the physical scars she was referring to.

'The physical pain was nothing compared to…' Greg let the words tail off. Abruptly he flung off the sheet that entangled their limbs and leapt out of bed. Picking up his discarded jeans, he slipped them on and stood by the window, looking out, his back towards Kirsty. There was something in the set of his shoulders that chilled her. She fumbled for the light switch. She needed to see his expression. But as she flicked the switch, nothing happened.

'The power's gone off,' Greg said. 'It happens often during storms. There should be a lantern here.' A few minutes later he found what he was looking for and lit the lamp, which cast shadows across the room. The storm was passing, the thunder now little more than a low rumble in the distance, and the lightning had stopped. When Greg eventually turned back to Kirsty his eyes were dark, his mouth set in a grim line.

'This was a mistake. I'm sorry, Kirsty. I should never have allowed it to happen.'

Kirsty could hardly believe what she was hearing. One minute he was holding her, making love to her, now he was looking at her almost as if he couldn't bear the sight of her.

'What do you mean, *allowed* it to happen? As far as I am aware, we both wanted it equally. And I don't—can't—regret it.'

'It's not fair on you. You were about to be married, Kirsty! Hell, no one gets over a love affair that quickly. If I had known…' He rubbed his scarred cheek in the gesture Kirsty was coming to know. 'It's too soon—for both of us. I can't be a replacement for Robbie. Ever.' His tone softened. 'You want more than I can offer. You deserve more than I can give.'

'And who gives you the right to decide what I need or want? Why don't we just let things develop between us? See where it takes us?' Kirsty drew her knees to her chest and pulled the sheet tighter around her. Suddenly she felt very vulnerable.

'That's precisely it, Kirsty. There is nowhere for this relationship to go. I can give you nothing. I can never, will never, fall in love or marry again. I will never have more children.'

Kirsty shivered as the blood turned to ice in her veins. 'For God's sake, Greg. It's your wife who is dead, not you.'

As soon as the words were out Kirsty could have bitten her tongue.

'Don't bring Kathleen into this.' Greg almost spat the words. 'It has nothing to do with her. I'm content the way I am. I like my life the way it is.'

Kirsty recoiled.

'And how is that, Greg?' she asked quietly. 'Empty, except for your work. You've mocked me for being afraid. But my fears are nothing compared to yours. I'm prepared to risk being hurt again. To take a chance. But you? You are afraid to live. And there's no fear worse than that.'

'I'll take my chances,' Greg said grimly. 'Don't you see? I could never give another woman everything she needs. I'm not like your ex-fiancé.

I wouldn't offer a woman half of me. It wouldn't be fair.' He looked at her bleakly, his eyes glittering as if they held raindrops. 'There is no future for us. Not ever,'

'We don't need to think of the future,' Kirsty said, desperate to convince the man in front of her. 'We could take one day at a time. Simply enjoy being together. See what happens from there.'

'And then what? You give up your career to stay with me here because, make no mistake, Kirsty, I will never leave Africa. And if you stayed I would have ruined another woman's life. And for what? For nothing.' He shook his head. 'I made that mistake once before, Kirsty, putting *my* needs, *my* career in front of those of the woman I loved, and what happened? I let her down in every way possible.'

There was no disguising the anguish in his eyes. Kirsty almost backed away from the naked pain she saw there. But instead she lowered her feet to the floor and, wrapping the sheet tighter, took a step towards Greg.

'I won't pretend that this…' she indicated the bed with a sweep of her hand '…meant nothing to me. I can't and you know that. Perhaps if I'd been able to pretend it didn't matter, you wouldn't be pushing me away.'

Greg strode across the room, closing the gap between them. Gently he tilted Kirsty's chin and looked deep into her eyes.

'Please, Kirsty. Let this go. It's for the best. You must believe me. I won't be responsible for ruining your life. I have ruined two lives already. The two people I loved most in the world. The two people I would have given my life for.' His voice was ragged with grief. He passed a hand across his forehead. 'I shouldn't have let this happen. You have every right to be angry with me. I had no right.'

Suddenly Kirsty was furious. She moved away from him.

'OK, you win. If you aren't ready to face life, with its risks and uncertainties, then you're not the man I thought you were.'

'That's just it. I am not that man—and I never will be.'

Kirsty was dismayed and embarrassed in equal measure. She had made a terrible mistake.

She had read much more into a simple case of lust than there had been. She should accept it for what it was. After all, it was the twenty-first century. Men and woman slept together for all sorts of reasons that had nothing to do with feelings. But she wasn't that type of woman. Never had been. Her heart and pride was still bruised after Robbie and it seemed both were to get another beating. At least sex with Greg had made her realise that what she had shared with Robbie was nothing compared to the short time she had spent in this man's arms. However, there was no point in prolonging this humiliating conversation.

'Well, it was fun while it lasted,' she said, trying to keep her voice light. 'If you don't mind, I'll wash then we can go to dinner. I don't know about you but I'm ravenous.' It was a lie, of course, but the last thing she wanted was for Greg to know how much he had hurt her. At the very least she needed to get out of the situation with a tiny bit of dignity still intact. She made her way towards the bathroom, hobbling slightly in the sheet that threatened to trip her up. *Please,*

God, don't let me fall she thought. *Even I can take only so much embarrassment.*

Behind her, Greg said quietly, 'I am sorry, Kirsty.'

'We made a mistake, that's all. Let's just pretend it never happened. We still have to work together and we are both grown-ups.' Kirsty winced as she closed the bathroom door behind her. What on earth had she gone and done?

A short time later Kirsty left their tent and wandered off to find the bar. Greg had already gone. The recent scene kept replaying in her mind. Despite everything he had said, she knew he had wanted her as much as she had wanted him. There had been no pretence in his response to her. Or had she completely misread the situation in the first place? Had she been the one who had unthinkingly pressed herself into his arms and raised her mouth to his? She felt her cheeks colour with mortification. Did he think she had seduced him? In which case, no wonder he wanted to put as much distance between himself and his hormonally rampant colleague as possible. She almost groaned with horror. But, she told herself, her reaction had been the normal response of a red-blooded female to a man she found sexy. And while she found him attractive, he was right—there was no way she needed another relationship with another man so soon after her disastrous engagement and certainly not with some one as emotionally repressed as Greg.

Finding herself at the bar, she accepted the drink that the barman thrust in her hand almost without thinking and gulped the cool beer down. The bar was simple, with one side completely open to the night air. Myriad candles and lanterns lit the space, flickering in the breeze. Outside a fire had been lit and several people sat around it, chatting and drinking. There were about a dozen other guests staying at the camp and most of them came up and introduced themselves to Kirsty before going on to describe what animals they had spotted that day. Kirsty caught a glimpse of Greg across the room. He was deep in conversation with a tall man with dark skin, and an elegant woman, who was dressed in a brightly patterned robe with a matching scarf.

Kirsty felt her heart thud as she caught his eye. He looked devastatingly gorgeous in his crisp, white, short-sleeved shirt and light-coloured trousers. Unwilling to hold his gaze, lest he read the shiver of desire that raced down her spine, she looked away. She was obviously still suffering the effects of a libido that was temporarily out of control. That was all, she told herself firmly.

The next moment Greg and his two companions were at her elbow and Greg introduced them. 'This is Nelson and his wife, Grace. They own this place. Nelson and Grace, Kirsty Boucher, a colleague and a, er, friend.'

'Any friend of Greg's is welcome here,' Nelson said, shaking Kirsty's hand. He turned to Greg. 'Why didn't you let us know you were coming?'

'I'd heard you were both out of the country. Besides, I didn't want special treatment. I knew if I let you know you'd have the staff pull out all the stops. You know when I come here I like to pay my way—and you always try and stop me.'

'Greg saved my wife's life,' Nelson told Kirsty. 'Back in the city. She had a brain aneurysm and luckily Greg spotted it. He operated and removed the clot.' He thumped Greg on the shoulder. 'Of course we'd do anything for him.'

'Nelson exaggerates,' Greg told Kirsty, looking embarrassed. 'I did no more than any doctor would have done. That was all.'

As the men continued to catch up, Grace pulled Kirsty to one side. She was one of the most beautiful women Kirsty had ever seen, with enormous brown eyes the colour of peat, fine chiselled cheekbones and a graceful neck adorned with beads.

'So are you only "friends"?' Grace quizzed Kirsty.

Kirsty nodded, unable to describe, even to herself, the nature of her relationship with Greg.

'Are you sure? Earlier—before you came in— it was as if he had been waiting for you, and then when you walked in, he only had eyes for you.'

Kirsty winced, her smile sad. 'You couldn't be more wrong.'

Grace didn't pry. 'Pity. I hoped for him there was more between you. He's such a wonderful person. He did save my life, you know,' she said quietly. 'And more. I was at university at the time. I could easily have been left brain damaged.

Instead, I finished my degree with honours. He was a fine neurosurgeon. One of the best.'

'What did you study?' Kirsty asked, grateful for the change of topic.

'Geography. Nelson and I met while we were studying. He was doing environmental law. Once we had finished we got married and came up here to start this place. It quickly became evident that there was a real shortage of medical facilities. When we heard what had happened to Greg, we persuaded him to take the position at the hospital.'

'You knew Greg before his accident?'

A cloud crossed Grace's face. 'We knew the whole family. It was awful what happened. Neither of us thought that Greg would ever recover. But coming out here to work seemed to give him a reason to carry on.'

'What was she like? His wife?' Kirsty couldn't help but ask.

'Kathleen?' Grace looked at Kirsty searchingly for a moment before seeming to read something in Kirsty's eyes that reassured her. 'She wasn't beautiful. Not in the way you are.' She ignored

Kirsty's shake of the head. 'But she drew people to her wherever she went. Whenever she was in a room it seemed to light up. She made people laugh. She was a wonderful mother and a good friend. We loved her. We loved them all. Greg was different when his family were still alive.'

'In what way?'

'Just different. Happier. More carefree.' She looked intently at Kirsty. 'But it's almost been five years and we think its time for Greg to move on. Find happiness once more. Perhaps fall in love. Get married again.'

'I'm pretty sure that's not what Greg wants.' Kirsty looked away from Grace's searching eyes. 'I don't think anyone will ever replace Kathleen.'

'No,' Grace sighed. 'I don't expect so. Not as long as Greg blames himself for the deaths of his family. Unless he accepts it wasn't his fault, that he was powerless to save them, I guess he'll always be alone. But tell me about yourself. What brings you to Africa?' As the two women chatted, Kirsty's thoughts kept straying back to Greg and what Grace had said. How could she have ever thought there could be something more between her and Greg than sexual desire? Not when it was clear to everyone that there would only ever be one woman for him.

Greg couldn't help himself. Despite his best intentions, his eyes kept straying back to Kirsty as she chatted with the other guests. Her auburn hair seemed to reflect the glow of the candles, making her face look paler than ever. He cursed under his breath. He had behaved despicably. He had made love to a woman who was on the rebound, who had recently broken up with her fiancé, for God's sake. If he had known he would never have given in to the raging lust that she inspired. Why did she have to be so beautiful? But he knew it wasn't simply her beauty. Kirsty made him feel alive for the first time in years. An unfamiliar sensation twisted his guts as he noticed that Kirsty was surrounded by a group of men who seemed to be hanging onto her every word. Surely he couldn't be jealous?

He'd had sex with other women since Kathleen had died, but those encounters had been different. He hadn't felt anything for them, or they for him.

Both parties had been happy to take what they'd needed and leave it at that. None of them had got under his skin the way Kirsty had. The thought shook him to his core. Was that what made him feel so bad? The fact that he had made love to Kirsty, not just had sex with her? That for the first time he had betrayed the memory of his wife?

He wandered off outside. He needed to be alone without the distraction of Kirsty hovering in the periphery of his vision. He looked up at the sky. Another storm was moving in and it was unlikely the power would be on any time soon. His thoughts turned inexorably back to Kirsty. What, in God's name, was he going to do about her? No doubt she believed him the worst kind of man and he deserved it. It didn't stop him wanting to make love to her again. He knew that as long as she was around it would be difficult to resist her—although after the way he had behaved he doubted that she would want anything to do with him.

He shook his head despairingly. When he had thought his desire for her had been an itch he'd just needed to scratch, how wrong he'd been.

Now he wanted her even more. Maybe they could have an affair, as Kirsty had suggested? See where it went?

But straight away Greg knew he couldn't. He hadn't been lying when he'd told Kirsty he'd never marry again or have more children. He felt the familiar stab of agony as he thought about his daughter. No, he would never allow himself to love again. Not when loving brought so much pain.

CHAPTER NINE

KIRSTY was woken up by a soft tapping. She was sitting up in bed when Greg came in. He looked rumpled, as if he hadn't slept much, and shadow darkened his jaw line. She wasn't surprised. He had insisted on sleeping in the car, and there couldn't have been much room for him to stretch his legs. Served him right, she thought viciously. As if she would have got up during the night and crawled into bed with him. When he'd suggested that he sleep elsewhere, it had been on the tip of Kirsty's tongue to tell him not to. Of course he shouldn't when there was a perfectly good bed in a separate room. But she hadn't. If he wanted to put as much distance between them as possible, that was fine by her.

'Its time for the drive, Kirsty,' he said, passing her a scalding cup of coffee. 'Take this. We'll get breakfast afterwards.' She accepted the coffee gratefully. At least he'd remembered that she couldn't function without a hit of caffeine.

It was still dark and cool as the open-topped Jeep rumbled down the track, stopping in front of their tent. Greg directed her into the seat at the rear of the Jeep behind the driver and guide, and climbed in beside her.

As his leg brushed against hers, Kirsty tucked the blanket Grace had thoughtfully supplied under her thighs. It wouldn't only serve to keep out the chill, it would provide a barrier between them because his proximity was stealing her breath.

She caught sight of the rifle resting against the front seat.

'It's not dangerous,' Greg had reassured her, noticing her eye the rifle anxiously. 'It's a precaution, that's all.'

But Kirsty's attention had shifted. 'What's that?' she asked, as the headlights caught the glitter of eyes in the shrubs.

'Wild dogs,' the driver replied, shifting into a lower gear as the Jeep started to climb a slope.

Taken by surprise, Kirsty couldn't stop herself from sliding into Greg. His arm came around her shoulders.

'Steady on, Mike,' he admonished. 'This isn't a rally.'

Kirsty tried to lift herself away from him but the angle was too acute. She was forced, ignominiously, to grip his thigh, the muscles bunching under her hand, and yank herself upright by grabbing her doorhandle. It came away in her hand. She fell against him again. She could feel his heart beating beneath her cheek. All she wanted to do was close her eyes and melt further into him. Resisting the impulse, she struggled once more to sit upright.

Greg looked at her in amusement, a wry smile tweaking the corners of his mouth. 'Give it up, Kirsty,' he whispered in her ear. 'We're almost there.'

And they were. The Jeep levelled out before coming to a slow stop beneath some wide-spreading acacia trees. Below them a dark pool of water glinted beneath fading stars as the sun's rays stretched tentative fingers to a lightening sky. Impala, warthogs and giraffe sipped at the water, only a few casting anxious glances for predators. Kirsty was enthralled—more so when a rhino with a calf made their ponderous way to the waterhole.

Mike's radio crackled. 'Over and out,' he ended, before turning the key in the ignition. 'Lion spoor further on. Let's see if we can track them.'

After trailing the spoor for almost an hour, Kirsty was thrilled when they came across a pride stretched out under a tree. Unthinkingly she reached out to Greg, grabbing his arm to get his attention. He looked down at her, grinning at her excitement.

'It's wonderful, isn't it, the first time you see them in their natural habitat?'

They watched for some time as the cubs played with their father who would reach out a large paw and swat them away from time to time. Eventually a lioness rose and padded away. The Jeep followed, keeping its distance downwind. After some time the lioness crouched in some deep grass and was hidden from their view. 'Over there,' Greg whispered to Kirsty, pointing at a herd of wildebeest in the distance. He handed Kirsty the binoculars and through their lenses Kirsty could see several young grazing close to the adults. Suddenly something seemed to startle them and they took off, heading in different directions. Kirsty swung her binoculars to find that the lioness had left her concealed position and was moving towards the herd at speed. She followed her with the binoculars and was horrified to find that a young wildebeest had become separated from the rest and the lioness was in full pursuit. She lowered the binoculars, unable to look any more. 'Oh, no,' she whispered. 'Somebody, do something. Fire in the air. Warn her off.'

Greg, too, had seen what was happening. He placed his hand over Kirsty's. 'We can't intervene. It's not fair on any of the animals.'

Within moments it was all over. The lioness had caught her prey. The other animals stopped running and soon went back to grazing some distance from the large cat. Kirsty was still aghast. 'It's too cruel,' she said. 'That poor animal.'

'It's life, Kirsty. She has to feed her cubs if they

are to survive. Death is a necessary part of the circle. We all know that.'

Kirsty looked at him. He was staring into the distance, his jaw clenched. 'Isn't it better,' he went on, 'knowing these animals have lived well before they died? Rather that than not live at all?' Kirsty wondered if he realised what he was saying. It was just a pity that Greg couldn't apply the same principles to his own life.

They took leave of the camp and Nelson and Grace a short while later, after sharing breakfast with them. While they ate, the couple shared their plans of setting up a small clinic for the local population, most of whom worked on the reserve. Greg and Kirsty joined in enthusiastically and Greg promised to return soon to help them with their plans. 'Come, too, Kirsty,' Grace pleaded. 'I feel we could be friends.' She looked from Greg to Kirsty before nodding complacently. As she kissed Kirsty goodbye, she whispered, 'Don't give up on him.' Kirsty didn't know what to say. Grace had simply got the wrong idea.

* * *

'Wait up for me, Kirsty, will you? I'm just about finished here,' Greg called out as she passed the surgical ward on her way back to her house. He was scribbling notes on the chart of a patient. For a moment hope flared. It died when he continued, 'There's a case I'd like to discuss with you if you, have a moment?'

Progress of another sort anyway. At least he was starting to take her medical skills seriously. 'Sure, Greg. I'll be outside.'

It had been a long day. While she waited for him she leant against the warm brick of the hospital wall, closed her eyes against the bright morning sun and breathed in the honeysuckle-scented fresh air. Although she tried to stop it, her mind kept flitting to Greg. The past couple of weeks, since the trip to the game reserve, had been both painful and difficult.

The journey back to the hospital from the game park had passed in silence. Kirsty had felt the tension between them almost like a physical force. But there had been little left to be said. Greg had made his position clear. As far as Kirsty was concerned, she had badly misjudged a man for the second time. She couldn't fight the ghosts of his wife and child. She knew that with chilling certainty.

And nothing in his behaviour since had led her to believe otherwise. When they had to work together, he was polite but distant. If he looked wan and haunted, it could only be because he was working too hard.

His footsteps brought her to the present. She pushed herself upright and greeted him with a tentative smile that matched his own.

They walked towards their accommodation immersed in conversation about the patient Greg had wanted to discuss. Since the trip to the reserve, the only conversations they'd had had been about medical cases.

Kirsty didn't notice the car parked outside their accommodation until they were almost there.

Greg looked at her. 'Expecting a visitor?' he asked.

'I don't know anyone here,' she said. 'Much more likely to be for you.' But then, to her astonishment, she recognised the tall, silver-headed man and his younger companion coming towards her.

'Dad! You could have let me know you were coming. And Robbie!' she added, glaring at him. 'What on earth are you doing here?'

'I'm presenting a paper at a conference in Cape Town,' her father said, bending down and kissing her cheek. 'So I thought a detour to see the situation here for myself would be a good idea. When he heard my plans, Robbie decided to come with me. We've come to take you home.'

'Take me home?' Kirsty echoed disbelievingly. *Over my dead body,* she thought grimly. She'd had just about as much as she could stand from men deciding her future.

'Kirsty, darling.' Robbie tried to reach out and hug her, but Kirsty stepped away from his arms. 'I told you on the phone I was coming.'

Kirsty was aware of Greg standing beside her, his expression grim. The easy camaraderie that had arisen between them while they'd discussed treatment options had disappeared as if it had never been.

'Dad, Robbie, this is my boss. Dr Greg du Toit. Dr du Toit meet my father and Robbie Knight.'

Greg shook their proffered hands. 'Pleased to

meet you both. Professor Boucher, if you'd give me a moment, I'll show you around. I'm sure Kirsty and Robbie have plenty to talk about.'

He turned towards her, lowering his eyelids too late to hide the brooding darkness she could only read as disapproval in his eyes. 'Kirsty, please invite your guests for dinner. I'll let Cook know to expect two more.'

At that moment Kirsty would have done anything to prevent Greg from leaving. Whatever else had passed between them, she could have done with his presence now. The last thing she wanted right now was to be left alone with Robbie. However, there was nothing for it but to let Greg leave.

'Come inside,' Kirsty said, as Robbie took the pile of case notes she had been planning to review that evening from her unprotesting grip. 'I'll show you around after we have a drink. And then I'm sure you'll want to get on your way before night falls.'

'On the contrary,' Kirsty's father said, 'I've got a couple of days free and Robbie here is planning to stay as long as it takes to persuade you to put this nonsense behind you and come home. And the sooner the better—the clinic can't survive too long with both of us away.'

'May I remind you that I never asked either of you to come? When I wrote to you about the desperate situation here, Dad, it wasn't because I wanted to be rescued. I simply thought you might be able to help—from the UK,' Kirsty said frostily. 'So, while you are welcome to stay the night, I'm too busy to act as hostess. Neither do I have any plans to "come home", as you put it.'

'I'll go and join Dr du Toit for that tour, shall I?' Keith Boucher said. 'Leave you two to talk.' And with that he beat a hasty retreat towards Greg. He'd always been good at avoiding emotional scenes, Kirsty thought ruefully. But what had brought him out here? Surely Robbie hadn't brought him along to help persuade her to return to him?

As Kirsty boiled the kettle she felt her temper rise. Her father and Robbie had no right to dictate how she lived. She whirled to find Robbie standing behind her, a contrite expression on his face.

'Think about what you are doing, Kirsty. How

can you bear it out here? It's all so primitive. Not your sort of place at all. Surely you can see that? Why can't you forgive me and come on home? I know it was a stupid thing I did. I'll never do it again, I promise you. It was just a final sowing of wild oats. It didn't mean anything. Let's just pick up where we left off.' He stepped towards her, a pleading smile on his face. Once that smile would have melted her, but that had been before… She left the thought unfinished. Better not go there.

'I'm not leaving here. At least for a while. And I'm certainly not coming back to you. Ever.'

'I know you're still angry with me and you have every right, but if I ever meant anything to you, you need to give us a chance,' Robbie persisted.

Kirsty whirled on him. 'No, I don't. You stopped meaning anything to me the moment you were unfaithful. For goodness' sake, Robbie. We were about to get married.'

All of a sudden the anger left her, replaced with sadness. Robbie would never know true love, she was certain. He would always be too wrapped up in his own needs. He wasn't a bad man, Kirsty knew now. Just a weak and selfish one.

'Let's leave it at that, Robbie. I'm happy here. Of course I was hurt and humiliated when I found you and Karen together. I couldn't bear telling everyone the wedding was off, particularly the reason why. I couldn't face their sympathy and I couldn't face you. But everything is different now. I don't love you any more. I'm not sure I ever did. You have to believe me when I say it's over.'

'I don't believe you. Unless…' Robbie's eyes narrowed suspiciously. 'Unless you've found someone else. That man Greg, your boss. What's he to you? They said when we arrived that the two of you were on some trip. I thought when they said it was with your boss, they meant someone a lot older.'

'It's got nothing to do with Greg.' Although as Kirsty said the words she wondered if they were true. 'Greg's not interested in me.' She couldn't quite keep the note of regret from her voice.

Robbie stepped closer, searching her eyes. Kirsty's gaze fell under his scrutiny.

'I'm right, aren't I? You do have feelings for him. That didn't take long.'

'Whether I do or whether I don't is no longer any concern of yours,' Kirsty reminded him, putting down her cup of coffee. 'Now, as far as I am concerned, this conversation is over. Shall we join my father and Greg on the wards?'

But his words had unsettled her. As they walked in silence towards the hospital, she thought of Greg, the strong planes of his face, the way he was with his patients, the way life seemed more exciting whenever he was around. She knew that in the short time she had been here she had changed. He had made her see that there was more to life than sports cars, new shoes and going out. She couldn't help but think what life would be like with Greg. It would always be an adventure. He'd never be satisfied with settling down in suburbia. He'd always be looking for new challenges and expecting the woman by his side to rise to those challenges, too. And then, with heart-stopping conviction, Kirsty knew that more than anything she wanted to be that woman.

The realisation made her head spin. She had never felt like this before. She glanced at Robbie. He had never made her go weak at the knees, never made her ache with need, the way Greg did. Robbie had never made her heart thud when she caught his eye across a room. But Greg did. With Greg she wanted nothing more than to be with him. Nothing else mattered. She would live in a tent in the desert if that's what it took to be with him. What she had felt for Robbie had been a pale imitation of what she felt for Greg. The truth hit her like a sledgehammer. She loved Greg. Completely, hopelessly and for ever.

But with equal certainty she knew that he would never love her. He was still in love with his Kathleen and *she* could never hope to compete with the memory of his dead wife.

Robbie was looking at her curiously. 'Are you all right? You look as if you've seen a ghost.' Kirsty almost laughed at the aptness of his description. Kathleen's ghost would always be there, between her and Greg. It was pointless to think there was any hope that Greg would ever allow himself to love her. All she would ever have was the memory of that brief interlude at the reserve. She shivered, wrapping her arms around her body.

'I'm OK.' She paused outside the paediatric ward. 'I think we'll find them in here.'

Sure enough, that was where they found them. The two doctors were bent over Mathew, deep in conversation. The little boy was sitting up in his cot, playing happily, his watchful mother by his side. Kirsty could barely look at Greg, scared he'd see her feelings written all over her face. She could have done with more time to collect herself.

'Professor Boucher—Keith—has shown a keen interest in Mathew,' Greg told them. 'In fact, he thinks he may be able to help.'

'I won't be certain until I make some calls, but I believe I might be able to persuade some of my colleagues at the hospital in Cape Town to let us use their facility to operate on this lad's face.' Kirsty was surprised. Although she had pleaded for his help in her letter, she hadn't really believed he would do anything. She had never known her father to do anything that didn't enhance his reputation or finances.

'That would be wonderful, Dad,' Kirsty said. 'If you could swing it?'

'If I can't then we'll operate here,' he said firmly. 'I have to say, Kirsty, this hospital of yours is exactly how you described it. Even the patients and staff. Greg introduced me to Jenny earlier on. She's a pretty tough cookie. Gave me quite a lecture about how the privileged should be doing more for the less fortunate.' Kirsty had rarely known anyone take her father to task and rarer still was the fact he had agreed to do something.

'I've got another patient I'd like you to see, Dad. You, too, Robbie,' Kirsty said, knowing that it was unlikely she'd get another opportunity to get her father's help.

Kirsty led the way to the medical ward. She opened the door to a side room. In it was a woman lying in a bed with a small child in her arms. Over the top of her sleeping child's head the woman looked at them in mute supplication, her brown eyes wide with fear. Kirsty knew that her father and Robbie wouldn't need to look at the woman's notes to know that she was dying.

'Thabisa here has end-stage AIDS. We have done all that we can, but sadly there is nothing left for us to do.' Kirsty reached over, tucking the blankets around the dying patient. It was so little. She took a deep breath, before going on. 'Her child has probably inherited the HIV virus but with the right treatment and drugs could go on to lead a productive life. Sadly, our supplies of the drug are limited. We need more, much more, if we are to ensure that every infected child has access. Furthermore, even if we do get the drugs we require, there are thousands of children in this country who have been left orphans. We need more homes for them, clothes, food and schools. The government is doing what it can, but there is so much need.' Kirsty struggled to keep her voice calm. She knew that any emotion on her part would weaken her argument in her father's eyes. She leaned over and touched the child's cheek with a finger, saying a few words of the African language she had been studying. She put her arms around the dying woman, gently lifting her into a position where she could manage a few sips of water. The woman smiled weakly, grateful for the small attention. Greg unwound his stethoscope and listened to the woman's chest. Wordlessly he shook his head at Kirsty.

Kirsty's father looked shocked. Robbie, on the other hand, appeared dismayed. Neither said anything until they had left the room.

'This is why you can't stay here,' Robbie said. 'Can't you see it's not your problem? Leave it to the government agencies who know what they're doing.'

'I can't accept that we can't do something. I won't accept it. What about your contacts, Robbie? Dad? Can't you persuade them to help?'

'Aren't you getting too involved, Kirsty?' her father asked. 'I think Robbie is right. Leave it to people who know what they're doing.'

'I don't think either of you know Kirsty as well as you think if you believe she'll give up on this,' Greg interjected quietly. 'And she's right. As doctors all we can do is stem the flow of the disease. It's a drop in the ocean. We can't just patch the children up and send them out to God knows what. It's easy to say there is nothing that can be done. But it doesn't absolve us from our responsibilities to our fellow human beings to try.'

Kirsty was surprised but pleased at Greg's intervention.

'I don't know what I can do, Kirsty. OK—operating on the child with the burns is one thing, and I can write you a cheque,' Keith offered.

'Any help you can give would be appreciated, of course, but I was thinking more of fundraising. You're always speaking at these large conferences, Dad.'

'So you mentioned in your letter, Kirsty. But I've never chosen to get involved in causes.'

'But there's no reason *you* couldn't, Kirsty,' Robbie interrupted. 'What about all these well-connected friends of yours? That's another reason for you to come home. You could do more back there than you ever could here. After all, it isn't as if you have much experience to offer out here.'

Kirsty felt as if she'd been slapped. She'd always known that Robbie didn't take her career seriously. He had often hinted that she could give up work once they were married. Not to stay at home with children—that he had made clear—

but to network with other wives, lay on dinner parties and in general help his career.

'I wouldn't say that,' Greg said quietly, his mouth set in a grim line. 'Kirsty has been an enormous help out here. Her patients and colleagues all think very highly of her medical skills and knowledge. She learns fast and has shown that she's more than prepared to roll her sleeves up and get stuck in.'

All eyes turned to Greg, as if they couldn't quite believe what they were hearing, Kirsty not least. It was the second time in the last half-an-hour that Greg had defended her and her clinical ability. Didn't he realise by now that she was perfectly able to stand up for herself?

'Let me think about it, Kirsty,' her father said. 'I'm not promising anything, but I will give it some thought. Now, if someone could point me in the direction of a shower and dinner? I don't suppose there's a decent restaurant in the vicinity?'

Kirsty and Greg shared a smile. 'No, I'm afraid not. But as I said earlier, you're both welcome to have dinner with us in the staff dining room. I've already alerted Cook that there'll be another two to feed. In the meantime, will you excuse me? I have some more patients I want to check on.'

By the time Kirsty and her two visitors made it to the staff house, the rest of the team was already waiting, drinks in hand. She introduced everyone as they took their seats, aware of the curiosity her visitors—particularly Robbie—were causing. Freshly showered, shaved and dressed casually but elegantly in trousers and sports jacket, he looked every inch the charming, successful surgeon he was.

They had almost finished dessert when one of the nurses came running into the room.

'Come quickly! There has been a bad accident. Two minibuses and many casualties.'

Jenny stood up. 'It's my shift.'

Sarah, Jamie and Greg stood, too. 'We'll help. Sibongele, could you take Calum home and stay with him, please?'

'I'll come, too,' Kirsty said, getting up from the table.

'Its OK, Kirsty, you stay with your guests. We'll cope,' Greg said, barely glancing in her direction.

'I'm coming, whether you like it or not.' Kirsty

had had enough of the men in her life talking about her and making decisions about her. And hadn't Greg just told her father that she was a useful member of the team?

Greg paused and looked as if he was about to protest. But something in her expression must have told him that she had made up her mind.

'OK, but stick with me,' he said

'Perhaps I can be of some assistance?' her father said, a spark in his eye. Kirsty couldn't remember seeing him look so animated.

'I suspect I'll only get in the way,' Robbie said. 'So I'll just head off back to your place, Kirsty, although if you need me, give me a shout.' He yawned and Kirsty wondered that she'd never realised how selfish he was until today.

'The door's open. Make yourself at home,' she tossed over her shoulder as she left the room.

The scene in the emergency room was chaotic. There were several patients with life-threatening injuries and many more with minor injuries re-quiring attention.

As they worked, more staff arrived from the nearby village to lend a hand. The crash had happened close to the village and a couple of nurses had rushed to the scene to help.

Another ambulance pulled up. 'These are the last of the casualties. One we had to cut out of the vehicle and the others are walking wounded. They can wait. But…' The nurse hesitated. 'One of the minibuses exploded. The veld is on fire. Many are trying to put it out but the grass is so dry. The wind is blowing it towards the village.'

'Make sure that the villagers are being evacuated. Has the fire service been called?' Greg demanded.

'Yes, but it will take them at least an hour to get here. I don't think it's going to be soon enough. The village will have burnt down by then unless the wind changes direction,' Jamie replied. 'Apparently Kirsty's friend—Robbie— has gone to help.'

Greg cursed under his breath. 'Idiot. He knows nothing about veld fires. They take hold so quickly and shifts in the wind can cause the fire to move behind you. Unless you know exactly what you are doing and have the right equipment, it's foolhardy to try and tackle them.' He must have noticed the alarm in Kirsty's eyes because he added hastily, 'I'm sure he'll be all right. The villagers will look after him.'

'I should go and find him,' Kirsty said. 'You don't know Robbie. He won't be told by anyone.'

'There's no way you're going anywhere near that fire,' Greg said firmly. 'They'll have enough to do keeping that boyfriend of yours safe without you adding to the problem.'

'I don't remember asking you for permission,' Kirsty ground out, trying to keep the fury and fear from her voice. 'I can't stop you ordering me about here, but you have no jurisdiction on me outside this hospital.' She pealed off her surgical gloves. 'Everything here is under control. The others can manage fine without me. So I'm going,' she held up a warning hand. 'And nothing you can say will stop me. I can drive myself. I don't need your help.'

'You can't go on your own, woman. See sense. The last thing we need here is to add you and Robbie to the list of casualties. Let the fire brigade handle it. You stay here and I'll go and make sure he's out of danger.'

'I'm coming, too,' Kirsty's father said quietly.

'He's my responsibility as much as anyone else's. But Greg's right, Kirsty. It's no place for a woman.'

'Stop it. Both of you.' This time Kirsty made no attempt to keep the anger from her voice. 'No more, do you hear? No more telling me what to do. I'm going and that's final. Whatever you choose to do is up to you.'

'Atta-girl,' Jenny cheered from across the room. 'You tell 'em. Too many men here think they're Rambo or some other kind of hero. Need a woman to keep them real.'

But Kirsty was out the door. Greg and her father looked at one another before shrugging and following her.

'We'll go in my car,' Greg said as he caught up with Kirsty. 'Or were you planning to walk?'

They piled into his vehicle in silence, Kirsty worrying about Robbie. Whatever had happened between her and Robbie, she'd had feelings for him once. She didn't want anything to happen to him.

As soon as they left the hospital grounds they could see the flames lighting up the sky over the village. The fire was bigger than anything Kirsty had ever seen or expected. She shivered.

'I hope the villagers are all right and that no one's been hurt. But their homes! They could lose what little they have.'

'The fire might still pass by the village,' Greg said, although Kirsty could tell from the tone of his voice that he didn't hold out much hope.

They reached the fire in less than five minutes, passing groups of people with their possessions balanced on their heads, hands hanging onto fearful children.

'They'll be planning to take refuge in the hospital overnight, or at least find space for the kids there,' Greg said. 'It's a warm night. At least if the adults do have to find shelter outside, they'll be OK.'

As they suspected, the flames had reached the perimeter of the village. A line of villagers stood flinging buckets of water on the fire, while others beat at the flames with coats or blankets—anything they could find. Kirsty could see immediately it was hopeless.

Greg pulled to a stop a safe distance away and

they spilled out of the car. Kirsty slung her medical bag over her shoulder and ran after Greg, determined to keep up with him as he ran down the main street. A fire engine had mercifully arrived, its flashing lights adding to the sense of chaos and urgency as the wind steered the fire ever closer to the fragile village homes. But, Kirsty thought, surveying the mayhem around her, one fire engine was unlikely to be enough.

She glanced over her shoulder to make sure her father was following, relieved to see that he was at least keeping a safe distance from the inferno that was raging around them. Sparks of burning debris floated in the swirling air, and the intensity of the smoke and heat caught in the back of her throat.

The hairs on the back of Kirsty's neck stood on end as ear-piercing screams split the air. She caught up with Greg as he stopped short, frantically scanning the mud huts to locate where the heart-wrenching sounds were coming from. Through the dense smoke, an older woman staggered towards them, her face streaked with soot and tears.

Her words were incomprehensible to both of

them, but her frantic pulling of Greg's arm and her pointing backwards towards a cluster of huts spoke of her urgency and desperation.

'I think she's trying to tell us someone's trapped back there,' Kirsty shouted to Greg, running forward. 'Come on!'

For a split second Greg stood immobilised by the wall of flames around them, the terror and confusion bringing that fateful night his family had died sharply into focus. He thought he could hear the cries of Kathleen and Rachel over the crackling flames. He remembered the heat of the fire, the flames licking his skin, the taste of smoke in his mouth, choking lungs. He hadn't been aware of it then, he had been too focused on reaching his family, but afterwards, night after night, the scene replayed in his mind. Could he have done more? Why had he left them alone? Every time he thought of that night he willed the outcome to be different. In his dreams he saved them, only to wake up, his heart crushed with the realisation of their loss. He had thought he couldn't bear it. Only immersing himself in work had saved him from going mad.

Gritting his teeth, he forced his mind back to the present. It was that night all over again. Could he bring himself to face the flames once more? He knew there was no choice. He was damned if anyone was ever going to die while he stood back and did nothing. Spurred on by a renewed sense of urgency and an anger that surpassed any fear, he ran after Kirsty as she darted into the labyrinth of pathways that snaked between the dwellings.

He grabbed Kirsty by the arm, spinning her towards him.

'Go back!' he shouted over the noise of the burning houses.

'No, I *won't.*' She shook herself free of his grip. The determination he saw there made his blood run cold. He knew that unless he picked her up and carried her back, she wouldn't go. For a split second he considered it, then another scream cut through the air. There was no time.

'Stay right beside me.' He had to lean close and shout in her ear to make himself heard above the sounds of the crackling flames. 'For God's sake, stay near me,' he beseeched her, not caring if she saw the fear in his eyes. He couldn't—wouldn't—lose her, too.

She saw the fear in his eyes and nodded mutely. Greg ran a finger over her lips before cupping her chin in his hands and pulling her against him. For the briefest moment she felt his lips touch hers and then he was off, running towards the huts.

Kirsty could feel her breath coming in gasps as she struggled to keep up with him, the thick, cloying smoke filling her lungs and stinging her eyes. Every now and again Greg would glance back to check she was following.

They emerged from the narrow path that skirted the village into a clearing. Most of the houses seemed to have been built around a circular space in the middle of the village. It was difficult to see through the smoke that hung over everything, but it looked to Kirsty as if most of the villagers had managed to flee in time. Greg was running from house to house, trying to locate the source of the screams.

Robbie emerged from the chaos and grabbed her arm, almost wrenching it out of its socket. She spun around, frowning in shock and bewilderment but relieved that he was safe. But where was Greg?

'Kirsty! No, don't!'

She struggled to free herself from his strong grip. 'I've got to, Robbie!' she yelled wrenching herself from his grasp. 'I can't just do nothing. I've got to help.'

'It's madness Kirsty. You'll get yourself killed.'

This was getting them nowhere, she thought in exasperation. Her eyes pleaded with him. 'Robbie, I know these people, I've got to help them.' She laid a hand gently but firmly on his. 'If you want to help me, please go help the others with the casualties.' And with that she turned on her heel and disappeared into the smoke.

Robbie stood transfixed, gazing after her until he could no longer see her. He dropped his arms to his sides, knowing it was futile to run after her.

'I should never have let you go…' he murmured to himself, as he turned back to help the others.

Kirsty's heart was beating so loudly in her ears she thought it was going to burst out of her chest. Her eyes darted around as she scanned the area frantically, trying to find Greg. *Where was he?* She suddenly felt completely alone and vulnerable in the cauldron of yellow and red flames. And then she saw him. He staggered from a hut, carrying a small child of about two and a bundle of rags in his arms. On closer inspection, Kirsty discovered, the rags were, in fact, a swaddled baby.

Greg thrust them both into her arms. 'Get them out of here now!' he ordered.

'What about you? Aren't you coming?'

'There's a young girl still inside. I'm going back for her. I couldn't carry all of them. Now go! There's not much time!'

'Greg!' She shouted but her words were whipped away by the roar of burning bush. Knowing that she had to get the children out of danger, she hitched the toddler onto her back where he clung to her neck, almost forcing the last remaining breath from her throat. She ran back as fast as she could, oblivious now to her aching lungs, intent on getting the children to safety. The toddler held on, coughing and crying, his mouth open in a perpetual wail of despair and fear. The baby lay worryingly inert and silent in her arms.

After what seemed an eternity but was probably only a few minutes, the smoke thinned and Kirsty burst through the haze.

Jamie and Sarah surged forward, gently taking the children from her and immediately laying them on the ground to examine them. For a moment Kirsty sank, exhausted, to her knees. Jamie looked over at Kirsty as he slipped an oxygen mask over the toddler's face. Sarah did the same with the baby.

'You could do with some oxygen, too, Kirsty,' Jamie said. 'Wait there and I'll get someone to see to you once I've seen to this little fellow.'

Kirsty shook her head. 'I'm fine. See to the children.'

'I'll be back as soon as I can, but in the meantime sit still,' Jamie said.

As he turned away, she staggered to her feet. Robbie darted forward, catching her before she fell. She struggled in his arms.

'Greg's still back there. I've got to help him.'

'Don't be a fool, Kirsty! You've done all you can,' Robbie said hoarsely.

She pushed against his chest but was too weak

to make any impact. Tears of exasperation and fear pricked her eyes. 'I can't leave him…'

Robbie studied her face for a moment, before realisation dawned on him. He had lost her for ever, he knew that now. Her heart belonged elsewhere. Sighing inwardly, he berated himself for being such a blind fool as to lose the one woman he had truly loved. Now it was too late. But at least now he could do something to repair the hurt and damage he had caused her.

'Your father's helping with the other casualties. I'll go look for Greg. You stay here and get seen to, OK?'

Kirsty looked up at him. She had almost no strength left to argue.

'I'm coming, too,' she said, getting to her feet.

Robbie ran a finger gently down her cheek. 'Leave this to me. Greg will be fine, don't worry.' Pulling off his shirt and soaking it in a bucket of water, Robbie held it over his mouth and ran back into the swirling nightmare of flames.

Taking a deep gulp of air, Kirsty followed Robbie back towards the burning houses where she had last seen Greg. Every breath brought a sharp pain in her chest. The smoke was thicker now and she could barely see. All of a sudden she tripped and went flying. She hit the ground with a thud and an excruciating pain jolted up her leg. Instantly she knew she had broken her ankle and Robbie was nowhere to be seen. The smoke muffled everything except the sounds of the fire around her. To her right the flames leapt closer with every second. Panicking, she looked around frantically for an escape route, but even had she found one she knew she'd be unable to escape the fire. With a sickening feeling in the pit of her stomach, Kirsty knew she had run out of time.

She tried to get to her feet, but when she put weight on her broken ankle she fell back to the ground. She bit back the screams of pain and horror that rose to her lips. Don't panic, she told herself. Whatever you do, don't panic. Spotting the branch of the tree which had probably caused her to lose her footing, she crawled towards it, biting down on her lip against the pain the movement caused in her foot. Inch by inch she moved towards the branch, convinced it was hopeless but refusing to give up.

When she reached it, she used it to lever herself off the ground.

If I can just take a few steps, she thought, if I can just stay alive for a few more minutes, he'll find me. She did not know where the certainty came from, but she knew deep in her soul that Greg wouldn't rest until he found her. All she had to do was help him find her.

'Greg,' she yelled as hard as her aching lungs would allow, 'I'm here, help me.' She manoeuvred the branch under her armpit and, using it as a crutch, took one painful step at a time. In front of her the flames had died a little having consumed all the dry grass there was to be had, and were now greedily making their way towards a small clump of trees to feed its hunger. But as faltering step followed faltering step, she knew she was too slow. Just as she was ready to give up and accept her fate, she heard Greg's voice calling her name. He sounded close.

'Over here. I'm over here,' she gasped. Tears from the smoke and fear ran down her cheeks.

'Hold on, Kirsty. I'm coming. For God's sake, hold on.'

Kirsty turned in the direction of his voice, almost blinded by tears and smoke. She hardly recognised Greg when he burst through the flames. Covered in ash, only his eyes were visible.

'Kirsty, thank God,' he cried as he crushed her in his arms. 'Are you all right?' He held her as she collapsed in his arms, relief robbing her of the last of her strength. She looked around frantically. 'Where's Robbie? Is he safe? You've got to find him.'

'He's fine. He's with the others.'

'My leg,' she whispered hoarsely. 'I think I've broken my ankle. I'm so sorry, Greg, for making you come after me.'

'Shh now,' Greg said, picking her up as if she weighed nothing at all. 'Did you think I'd let anything happen to one of my doctors?'

And that was all she was, Kirsty thought as her eyes closed. Just one of his doctors. Another responsibility. As she lost consciousness, she was unaware of Greg's lips on her hair.

'Don't leave me,' he murmured. 'Don't you dare leave me, too.'

CHAPTER TEN

Kirsty woke up to find herself in one of the hospital beds. Images from the night before flashed in her head. She remembered Greg picking her up in his arms. After that she must have floated in and out of consciousness as she had been placed on a stretcher and put in an ambulance. She could recall being given oxygen, her ankle being X-rayed and someone's gentle hands wrapping her ankle in a cool, soothing cast. Her father's face had drifted in and out as had the faces of Jamie, Sarah and Jenny. But she couldn't recall Greg's presence. Or Robbie's. Were they all right?

She tried to sit up, fighting the fear that gripped her and weight of the bedclothes pinning her down. She had to find out.

As she struggled someone pressed her gently

back into the pillows. Her eyes flickered open and her heart soared. It was Greg. Despite the bandage on his right hand and singed eyebrows, he was here, in one piece. Thank God. Regardless of how he felt about her, she knew she'd be happy as long as he was in the world. Unbidden and deeply resented tears washed her eyes.

'Greg…' was all she could manage through her aching throat.

His voice was husky. 'Hey, hey, take it easy. You're safe now. You won't be walking without crutches for a while, but otherwise you'll be out of here by tonight.'

'Robbie—what about Robbie!' she asked grasping Greg's wrists. 'Is he OK?'

Greg flinched before smiling down at her. 'He's fine, too. Jamie's giving him a final once-over, then you'll be able to see him.'

He disengaged Kirsty's hands from his wrists.

'I'll tell him you were asking for him when I see him. Your father's just outside. He wants to see you, but I've limited him to five minutes only. You need to rest some more before I'm prepared to give you the all-clear.' He paused, and it looked as if he was about to touch her, but instead he rammed his fists deep in his pockets. Despite the events of the night before, it seemed as if he intended to keep his distance.

Greg left the room as her father entered.

'How are you, Kirsty?' her father asked softly, looking down at her. For the first time in as long as she could remember his eyes were tender. She had rarely seen him looking so subdued. He seemed uncomfortable.

'I'm perfectly fine. I don't know why everyone is making such a fuss.'

'Perhaps because they are fond of you? You seemed to have made quite an impact in the short time you've been here.' He shuffled his feet. 'I'm very proud of you, Kirsty. I hope you know that. I know I haven't been around very much for you since your mother died, and I wanted to say how sorry I am. She would have been so proud of you, too.'

He cleared his throat. 'You remind me so much of her.'

The rare display of emotion touched Kirsty deeply. She reached out for his hand. 'I do? I miss her, too, Dad. And I've missed you as well.' Kirsty felt the familiar ache, thinking of her lost childhood. She swallowed the lump in her throat. She had to try and reach her father one last time. 'I always wondered if you were sorry it wasn't me that died in the accident. Sometimes it seemed as if you could almost not bear the sight of me.'

Keith looked horrified and then ashamed. 'I am so sorry. I know I was weak and selfish, but every time I looked at you, I saw your mother. You were always so much like her—and not just in looks.' He leaned over Kirsty and tucked a strand of hair behind her ear. 'When she and your sister died, I thought my life was over. The only way I could deal with missing them was to throw myself into my work. The only time I didn't think of them was when I was working. All I wanted was to come home too exhausted even to dream of them. And there you'd be, refusing to go to sleep until I had tucked you in. Wanting to tell me all about your day. Everything you'd done. Making demands when I'd exhausted myself with the effort of forgetting.'

'I was desperate to make you notice me. I

wanted to make you proud of me, but you never seemed to care. You never once came to prize-giving, even in my final year when I won all those prizes. Why, Dad? I was so alone. I missed them, too. I needed you more than ever.'

'I don't expect you to ever forgive me, Kirsty. As you got older you stopped telling me things. I know it was my fault that a chasm had opened up between us, but by the time I realised how far apart we were, it was too late. You had your own life, university and your career. I didn't know how to get close to you again. But I was always so proud of you. That fierce determination to succeed. Your ability to stand on your own two feet. You did all that by yourself, Kirsty—you are so much stronger than you think.'

Kirsty smiled. 'I know that now, Dad. Being out here has taught me that at least. Life no longer holds any fears for me—not even being alone. I suspect now that was the reason I thought myself in love with Robbie. I wanted so much to belong somewhere.'

'And now?' her father asked gently. 'You know you'll always have a home with me. We can start to get to know each other properly. Spend time together. I know I have no right to be part of your life, but if you'd let me—I'd be grateful.' He looked at her and Kirsty could see that he meant every word.

'I'd like that, Dad.'

Her father squeezed her hand. His look of relief told Kirsty how much it had cost him to open up and expose the wounds that lay beneath the austere surface.

'By the way, that Jenny woman is something else,' he said admiringly. 'She gave me a real rollicking about my apparent selfishness and my parental obligations. Anyway, it seems as if I have agreed to set up an exchange programme with one of the teaching hospitals in Cape Town for some of the patients here to be treated free of charge. I'll give them some of my time on a regular basis in return. What do you think? It means I'll be coming out to Africa on a regular basis. We'll see much more of each other and more of the patients will be getting the specialist care they need. Perhaps it will go some way towards making things up to you?'

'You shouldn't do it just because of me, Dad,' Kirsty said.

'You're not the only one who has learnt something out here, my girl. What matters…' His voice wavered. 'Is I have my daughter back. And medicine has given me so much, it's about time I gave something in return. After all, it's why we all trained, isn't it? To make a difference.'

'Then I think it's a great idea. Thank you.'

Father and daughter smiled at each other. Kirsty felt her heart shift. Something good had come out of her time in Africa. It would take time for her and her father to learn to know each other properly—but it was a start.

'Have you seen Robbie?' she asked, changing the subject.

'Yes, I have. I rather think he's enjoying being the centre of attention. He's told me it's really over between you and why. I gather he is planning to leave tomorrow morning,' Keith replied, pulling up a seat. 'Will you be very sorry to see him go?'

'No, Dad. Really. Robbie and I have had a narrow escape in more ways than one. I was never the right woman for him nor him the man for me.'

'Is it Greg? He's got something to do with this, hasn't he?' Keith asked. 'I can see why you'd find him attractive in a rough sort of way. And he's one hell of a doctor. You look at him the way your mother used to look at me. My God,' he said, realisation dawning. 'You're in love him, aren't you?'

'Yes, but it's no use. He doesn't want me.'

Keith looked at her disbelievingly. 'Doesn't want you? Are you sure about that? You should have seen him when he realised you'd gone back into the fire. I suspect he would have happily knocked Robbie to the ground for not stopping you, had there been time. No, I think you're mistaken there.'

'There's other complications, Dad. Trust me. There's no future for us,' Kirsty said, closing her eyes wearily. 'I think I'll just rest for a while, if that's OK.' And before she knew it she had drifted off into a deep sleep.

When she next woke up, Greg was back. He had showered and changed and, apart from the bandage, he looked as he always did. Kirsty felt her heart squeeze. She knew she'd have to leave Africa. She didn't think she could bear to be around Greg—loving him but never being able to have him. But the thought of leaving him and the people who had begun to mean so much was almost too much to bear.

'I have someone to see you,' he said softly, and stood aside.

Robbie too had showered and changed, but he looked uncharacteristically disheveled, as if the night's events had taken their toll. 'I had to make sure for myself you were all right. For God's sake, Kirsty, what on earth got into you? You could have been killed.'

'But I wasn't. Although I'm sorry I put anyone else in danger.' She glanced over at Greg who was standing with his arms folded. He looked grim.

'I'll leave you two alone,' he said abruptly. 'I'm sure there are things you want to say to each other.'

'Please, don't go,' Kirsty said quickly, but he was already pushing the door open. 'There's nothing Robbie and I have to say to one another that you can't hear.'

Greg shook his head, his eyes expressionless as he looked at her. 'I'd rather not,' he replied, and left.

His departure sent a chill through Kirsty. Did he think she and Robbie were going to have a lovers' reunion? she wondered in despair. If she had the energy, she'd get out of bed and run after to him to explain. But what was the point? He had made it all too clear that there was no future for them.

Suddenly aware that Robbie was saying something to her, she dragged her attention back to him as he leant over the bed and kissed her on her cheek. 'Do you forgive me?' he asked.

Kirsty's eyes met his. *How could I have thought I was once in love with Robbie?* she asked herself, noting his hangdog expression which in the past used to make her go weak at the knees. Now, she realised, it just made her pity him all the more.

Kirsty managed a small smile. 'I do, Robbie. It's all in the past now.'

He leaned over, clasping her hand. 'Is there any chance we could…?'

'No.' Kirsty shook her head and gently disengaged her hand. 'If we had been right for each other, you would never have cheated on me. And if I had loved you enough, we would have found some way to have made it work.'

Robbie stood up, his expression regretful. 'I was stupid and I guess I'll have to live with the consequences.'

'I suspect it won't be long before you've forgotten all about me.'

'And you'll be wrong.' He hesitated. 'I'll see you soon? Back in the UK?'

'Yes.'

'Goodbye, then, Kirsty,' he said quietly, kissing her gently on the forehead. 'You'll always be in my heart, no matter what you think.'

'Goodbye, Robbie. Look after yourself.' Despite what had happened, she hoped he'd find happiness one day.

Robbie took a deep steadying breath as he walked down the corridor. He could hardly believe that he had lost Kirsty for good. Deep down he had been sure he could win her back. How wrong he'd been. What a fool he'd been. But there was something he had to do before he left tomorrow.

He eventually found Greg outside in the hospital gardens. For a second he doubted the wisdom of what he was about to do. What if he was wrong? No. Robbie straightened his shoulders. Being out in Africa, even for this short time, had made him a better man. It was time he started acting like one.

Greg looked round as Robbie approached. He nodded at him. 'Did you and Kirsty sort everything out then?' he asked tersely.

'Yes, we did.'

The muscles in Greg's jaw tensed. He stared out over the horizon. 'So she'll be joining you back in the UK, then?'

Robbie paused. He hoped he was doing the right thing. 'You know, Greg,' he said softly, 'some people go through their whole life never finding that special someone. Someone mentioned you lost your wife and child some years ago. I can't even begin to imagine how hard that must have been for you, but you were damn lucky to have had a love so special the first time round.'

Greg glowered at him. He didn't have to listen to this. 'It's none of your damn business. I know how blessed I was—I don't need you of all people to remind me. I trust *you* appreciate what you've got.' Greg turned on his heel. 'I hope you'll both be very happy.'

Robbie grabbed his arm, ignoring the dangerous narrowing of Greg's eyes. 'I lost my chance of happiness. I threw it away. Kirsty and I are over for good. The way is clear for you.'

Greg's heart slammed in his chest. For a moment happiness flooded his body, only for it to be dispelled a second later. What was the use? he thought, raking his hand through his hair. 'I can't…' His eyes were anguished.

'Can't…or won't?' Robbie demanded, suddenly frustrated. 'I know how you feel about Kirsty, and it's taken every ounce of my nerve to come out here to talk to you. Do you think this is easy, trying to persuade another man to make the woman I love happy?' Robbie shook Greg's arm gently, his tone softening. 'Would your late wife really want you to punish yourself for the rest of your life?'

Greg raised his eyes. The question had never occurred to him. 'No, she wouldn't,' he answered after a while.

Of course she wouldn't. He could imagine what she'd say if she knew how hard he'd being trying to hide from life. She of all people would have wanted him to move on. Find happiness wherever, however he could. But was it too late? He knew he had hurt Kirsty badly. Could she ever forgive him? There was only one way to find out.

'Well, then?' Robbie half smiled. 'Don't you think it's time you stopped punishing yourself?' He clapped Greg lightly on the shoulder, leaving him alone with his thoughts.

Greg stole into Kirsty's room, careful not to wake her. He quietly pulled up a chair alongside her bed and sat down, resting his forearms on his thighs. In the dim overhead light he noticed how her long lashes cast shadows on her cheeks, her long hair framing her delicate features. He thought she had never looked more beautiful.

Almost as if she had sensed his presence, Kirsty slowly opened her eyes. She smiled sleepily when she saw him.

'Hi, you,' she murmured.

'Hi, you, back.' His voice was soft. 'How are you feeling?'

Kirsty turned over on her side to face him, her hand resting under her cheek. 'Much better, thank you,' she replied politely. She paused. She would have to tell him sooner rather than later. 'Greg…I'm going to go back to the UK.'

Greg frowned, startled. 'To be with Robbie?'

'No. Not in the way you mean. I guess we'll always have contact. Especially as he works for my father. But as I said before, Robbie and I are over. What love there was….' She left the words unfinished. 'But I *am* going to leave. I'm not much use here, not with this cast on. So I may as well go back.' Although she tried, she couldn't keep the sadness from her voice.

'Are you certain it's over between you and Robbie? Out there in the fire, when you thought he was in danger… And then when you woke up, he was the first person you asked for. Are you sure there's no hope of getting back together? He stills love you.'

'But I don't love him.'

'Perhaps given time?' Greg persisted.

Kirsty finally lost her temper. 'Greg du Toit, you have no right to interrogate me about my love life. I can see why it might make you feel better to believe that Robbie and I still have feelings for one another. It lets you off the hook.' Seeing he was about to protest, she held up an admonishing finger. 'You have made it perfectly clear that you and I have no future. I accept that. Now, once and for all, butt out of my life. Besides…' she glowered at him '…aren't you needed elsewhere?'

'I'm exactly where I need to be,' Greg said, his eyes sparkling. 'With one of the most difficult women I have ever met or ever want to meet. And I have no intention of leaving her again.'

Kirsty's heart thudded.

Greg slid onto the bed beside her and pulled her close. She smelt the same lemony aftershave, and felt the muscular hardness of him.

'I've been such a fool,' he groaned. 'When I almost lost you, I knew I couldn't live without you. But then you seemed frantic about Robbie. And I thought it was too late.'

'And Kathleen? What about her?'

Greg pulled her closer. 'I loved Kathleen and part of me will always love her. I thought I didn't deserve happiness again. It was my fault that she and Rachel died. What kind of man doesn't protect his family?' Kirsty made to interrupt him, but he held a finger to her lips. 'Let me tell you, while I can. The grief and the guilt almost destroyed me. I felt I didn't deserve happiness. And then you came into my life. You, with your odd mixture of vulnerability and sophistication. I tried so hard not to fall in love with you, but it was no use. I tried to tell myself that it was just lust. And then we made love and I knew I could never get you out of my mind. It was the worst kind of hell, Kirsty—believe me. Wanting you, but feeling as if it was so wrong, as if it were the worst sort of betrayal to fall in love again.'

'Well, thank you very much. I can assure you I didn't plan any of this either,' Kirsty muttered under her breath. She couldn't make out what he was trying to tell her. Something about not wanting to fall in love with her. Something about not succeeding. She felt a small surge of happiness, followed sharply by a needle of exasperation. How did he feel about her? And what—if anything—was he going to do about it?

'And then there was the thought of you sacrificing your career to be with me,' Greg went on. 'It was Kathleen and I all over again. I couldn't let it happen.'

'It isn't entirely up to you, Greg,' Kirsty said crossly. 'Do you think for one moment I wanted to fall in love so soon after being engaged? And with a man who really still belongs in the Dark Ages? Do you think for one moment I planned to fall in love with someone who lives in deepest Africa, as far away from civilisation as you can get?' Kirsty took a deep breath, ready to continue to list all the reasons she had never intended to fall in love with him, but he stopped her words with a finger on her lips again.

'What did you just say?' he asked, his eyes glittering.

'I said it wasn't in my plans to fall in love with a man and have to start a new life, particularly a man as impossible as you…'

But once again Kirsty was stopped in full

flight—this time as Greg brought his lips down on hers. 'Let's stop at the bit where you said you loved me,' he said, once he had kissed her soundly. 'The rest can wait until we both have our strength back.' He released her. 'I shouldn't overtire you. You need to rest.'

'For God's sake, Greg. There you go again. Don't you know by now I'm stronger than I look? We're going to finish this conversation right here. I want to know what happens now.' Greg gathered her in his arms again, and rested his chin on top of her head.

'Last night—the fire. At first I was terrified. The smoke, the flames. It brought it all back to me. I felt paralysed with fear. But you didn't hesitate. You were so brave—but reckless, too.' He couldn't resist admonishing her. He would much rather she had stayed safely away from the fire, but then she wouldn't be the woman he adored.

'And then when no one knew where you were, only that you had gone back in, I thought I was about to lose the woman I loved all over again.'

Kirsty turned towards Greg so she could look him in the eyes. She felt her throat close at the naked pain she saw there. Reaching up, she kissed his eyes as if her touch could take away his anguish.

'But you saved me. You rescued that woman and her children. Robbie, too.'

'I think it's the other way round. You and the fire saved *me*. In some way it felt as if I had been released from my burden of guilt. In some small way I had paid back the debt I owed my wife and child. I'll never forget them, Kirsty. They will always be part of me, but if you are prepared to take the risk, prepared to spend your life with a stubborn fool…'

Happiness soared through Kirsty's veins. Whatever it took, she knew she wanted nothing more than to spend the rest of her life with this man. But she needed to hear the words.

'What exactly are you saying, Greg?' she asked, a small smile playing on her lips.

'I love you and want to marry you. Isn't it bloody obvious?' he said tersely. 'But if it's too much or not enough, I'll understand.'

'You mean I'll have to stay with you here? In this country? Without access to my beloved shops?

Hmm, let me see,' she teased. But from the look in Greg's eyes she knew he needed an answer.

'Of course, Dr du Toit. You know I always like to do as you ask.' She had just enough time to see his eyes glow before he brought his lips down on hers and she knew at last she was exactly where she belonged—for good.

MEDICAL™

Large Print

Titles for the next six months...

March

SHEIKH SURGEON CLAIMS HIS BRIDE Josie Metcalfe
A PROPOSAL WORTH WAITING FOR   Lilian Darcy
A DOCTOR, A NURSE: A LITTLE MIRACLE Carol Marinelli
TOP-NOTCH SURGEON, PREGNANT NURSE Amy Andrews
A MOTHER FOR HIS SON   Gill Sanderson
THE PLAYBOY DOCTOR'S MARRIAGE   Fiona Lowe
PROPOSAL

April

A BABY FOR EVE   Maggie Kingsley
MARRYING THE MILLIONAIRE DOCTOR   Alison Roberts
HIS VERY SPECIAL BRIDE   Joanna Neil
CITY SURGEON, OUTBACK BRIDE   Lucy Clark
A BOSS BEYOND COMPARE   Dianne Drake
THE EMERGENCY DOCTOR'S   Molly Evans
CHOSEN WIFE

May

DR DEVEREUX'S PROPOSAL   Margaret McDonagh
CHILDREN'S DOCTOR,   Meredith Webber
MEANT-TO-BE WIFE
ITALIAN DOCTOR, SLEIGH-BELL BRIDE   Sarah Morgan
CHRISTMAS AT WILLOWMERE   Abigail Gordon
DR ROMANO'S CHRISTMAS BABY   Amy Andrews
THE DESERT SURGEON'S SECRET SON   Olivia Gates

MILLS & BOON®
Pure reading pleasure™

0209 LP 2P P1 Medical

MEDICAL™

Large Print

June

A MUMMY FOR CHRISTMAS	Caroline Anderson
A BRIDE AND CHILD WORTH WAITING FOR	Marion Lennox
ONE MAGICAL CHRISTMAS	Carol Marinelli
THE GP'S MEANT-TO-BE BRIDE	Jennifer Taylor
THE ITALIAN SURGEON'S CHRISTMAS MIRACLE	Alison Roberts
CHILDREN'S DOCTOR, CHRISTMAS BRIDE	Lucy Clark

July

THE GREEK DOCTOR'S NEW-YEAR BABY	Kate Hardy
THE HEART SURGEON'S SECRET CHILD	Meredith Webber
THE MIDWIFE'S LITTLE MIRACLE	Fiona McArthur
THE SINGLE DAD'S NEW-YEAR BRIDE	Amy Andrews
THE WIFE HE'S BEEN WAITING FOR	Dianne Drake
POSH DOC CLAIMS HIS BRIDE	Anne Fraser

August

CHILDREN'S DOCTOR, SOCIETY BRIDE	Joanna Neil
THE HEART SURGEON'S BABY SURPRISE	Meredith Webber
A WIFE FOR THE BABY DOCTOR	Josie Metcalfe
THE ROYAL DOCTOR'S BRIDE	Jessica Matthews
OUTBACK DOCTOR, ENGLISH BRIDE	Leah Martyn
SURGEON BOSS, SURPRISE DAD	Janice Lynn

MILLS & BOON®
Pure reading pleasure™

0209 LP 2P P2 Medical